THE GREAT DODO COMEBACK

Fiona Sandiford
illustrated by Clare Elsom

USBORNE

Contents

CHAPTER ONE

Popcorn

Leni loved birds of every kind. Big and small, chirpy and squawky, wide-winged and web-footed. They were all special.

In her notebook, Leni liked to draw pictures of different birds she'd spotted, note down any distinctive calls, and copy the tracks she noticed in the sand.

Leni was a happy mix of down-to-earth and up-in-the-clouds. She had owl-brown eyes and raven-black hair, which usually had leaves stuck in it, because she spent so much time in her tree house.

It was from here that Leni gazed out towards the horizon, where the ocean blended into the sky like a big blue slushie. This afternoon she was looking for seabirds, diving down to the water to catch fish. But suddenly a flapping of wings interrupted her view and, in a flurry of green feathers, a bird landed on the windowsill.

"Oh, Popcorn, it's you!" cried Leni.

Popcorn was an echo parakeet, a rare type of parrot found only in Mauritius, an island country in the Indian Ocean.

Mauritius was Leni's home and she was fond of all the birds here, but especially Popcorn. A wild parakeet, he lived in a nearby tree, but he liked to follow her around, listening to what was being said and joining in from time to time.

Leni held Popcorn in her hand and stroked him. She touched her nose to his red beak.

"Hey, Popcorn, are you hungry?"

"Hungry!" the bird squawked. He loved to copy human speech. Leni smiled, cut open a pomegranate and offered him half in her open palm. The parakeet sat on her hand, and started pecking at the seeds as delicately as if he were picking flowers.

Leni lived with her mum and dad on Mauritius's main island, in a place called Baie de la Vie, which means "Bay of Life" in French. This beautiful, palm-fringed bay looked out over a clear blue lagoon and coral reef. Leni's mum, Manishi, and dad, Roshan, owned some thatched holiday huts dotted along the shore and rented them out to visitors.

Near the beachside huts stood the large and majestic "dodo tree" and in its branches nestled the tree house, which Leni's father had built for her when she was six years old.

Popcorn was just finishing his pomegranate when Leni heard voices outside. "Wonder who that is?" she said to the bird. The huts were quiet at the moment. In fact, there were no guests staying in any of them and the neon "vacancy" sign glowed every night outside the front gates.

Leni peered down and spotted her father walking towards one of the holiday huts. He was carrying an old, battered travel trunk by one of its leather handles. Behind him, holding the other handle, was a new guest.

It looked like somebody had checked in.

CHAPTER TWO

The Handkerchief

The new arrival was an old man. He was slim, with spindly arms and legs and had rolled up the sleeves of a shirt that was brownish, but probably used to be white. In contrast, his hair was white, but probably used to be brown. From her tree house lookout, Leni could see he hadn't put on any sunscreen, and his bald spot was pinker than a flamingo's tongue.

The old man had a white moustache, was wearing a pair of well-worn sandals and had a hanky hanging out of his back pocket. "The trunk is a bit of a beast!" he remarked as they hauled it onto the front deck of hut 187.

Just why it was numbered 187 had never been clear to Leni, as there were only five huts for holidaymakers. But anyway…

"Here you are, sir, number 187," said her father cheerfully. He took out a key and unlocked the door of the hut. Together they hauled the trunk inside and then reappeared at the front door.

"Thank you so much," the man said to Leni's dad in an English accent.

"Don't mention it," replied her dad. He handed the old man the key. "Your hut will be cleaned every day by our wonderful cleaners, Marion and Mimi. They'll also take care of any laundry you'd like done. Anything else you need, just use the phone in your hut and we'll be right over to help."

"Thank you, that is most kind," said the old man.

"Enjoy your stay, sir," her dad said. Then he smiled and waved goodbye.

The white-haired man waved and returned to his hut. As he did so, his handkerchief fell out of his back pocket. But he didn't notice and closed the door behind him.

Leni climbed down from the tree house, padded across the sand and picked up the hanky. It was cotton and crumpled. She unfolded it carefully and held it by the corners.

"Look at that," she said under her breath. On one corner of the hanky, there was a little embroidered blue owl and the initials IBBB.

"Look at that," repeated Popcorn.

"IBBB? I wonder what that means," she whispered to her companion.

Leni hesitated, wondering whether she should knock on the old man's door. "He's only just arrived. Is it a good idea to disturb him?" she asked the bird. Then she sighed and said, "Oh well, I'll knock anyway. Even if it's not."

Popcorn just looked at the hanky.

"Snot!" he squawked.

CHAPTER THREE
Larking About

Leni could feel Popcorn's little claws digging into her shoulder as she knocked on the door of hut 187.

Somewhere inside a toilet flushed. This was followed by the sound of footsteps approaching. Then the door opened.

"Good day, miss," said the old man politely.

Closer up, Leni could see his eyebrows were scant and wispy, and as white as the clouds above.

"Hello, sir," replied Leni. "You dropped this outside." She held out the hanky.

"Oh, thank you, young lady. That is very kind of you,

very kind indeed," said the man, taking it and wiping his damp hands.

"Kind indeed," repeated Popcorn, in a clipped English accent.

"Ha ha ha ha!" the man laughed. "A perfect imitation!" Then, he reached into the chest pocket of his shirt and pulled out a pair of spectacles. He wiped them with the hanky, put them on and studied Popcorn more closely. "Your bird there," he said, "is it a Mauritian parakeet?"

"Yes, it is," replied Leni. "His name is Popcorn."

"He's a most fine creature," continued the man in admiration. "Splendid beak, wings and tail feathers... Mauritian parakeets are rare, you know. They're the only type of parrot in these parts that's not become extinct."

Leni nodded. "And he copies whatever you say."

"Hmm, whether you want him to or not, I assume?" said the old man.

"I assume!" pronounced the bird with an impeccable English accent.

"What a treat!" cried the man. Then, looking at Leni

he said, as if to explain, "Oh, do excuse me, I'm a bit of a bird nerd."

"I did notice the owl on your hanky," she admitted.

"Oh yes, that," said the man. He flapped the hanky and then stuffed it back into his pocket. "Please allow me to introduce myself. My name is Professor Jethro Flowers and I work at the Institute of British Bird Brains."

So *that* was what the initials stood for, thought Leni — Institute of British Bird Brains.

"And you are?" enquired Professor Flowers.

"Um, my name's Leni," she replied. "My parents are the owners here. You just met my dad."

"Roshan? Oh yes, a most welcoming man."

"I really love birds too. But I'm not a professor...yet," Leni said.

"Aaaah, a fledgling!" smiled Professor Flowers.

"I suppose so," said Leni. "Actually, when I grow up I want to be a vet. I want to help sick and injured birds. That's my dream."

"A splendid one too!" remarked the professor. "You'll spread your wings. All in good time."

"I've read every book on birds that I can and I love watching the wild birds around here. From my tree house." She pointed to the dodo tree. Professor Flowers squinted to see the tree house, tucked up in the branches.

"What a fine lookout," he said.

"Go on, test me," Leni challenged him. "Ask me questions about bird ailments."

"Anything?" asked the professor.

Leni nodded. "Anything."

The professor's eyebrows arched as he thought. "All right then," he said, stroking his chin, "Doctor Leni, how would you treat an albatross with muscle strain?"

"I'd give it a pill to deal with the pain," she replied.

Professor Flowers laughed.

"A guinea fowl with a case of the bloat?"

"Open wide and I'll look down your throat."

"A jungle bush quail who's got a sore beak?"

"Take antibiotics — over a week."

The professor was having fun and he kept going.

"A flamingo who's tripped up and broken a bone?"

"Splint the leg 'til he can walk on his own."

"An emu who's lost all its zeal and zest?"

"A medical check-up and full blood test."

"Ha ha, fantastic!" laughed the professor. "Not much ruffles your feathers does it, young Leni? And you're as sharp as an eagle's talon. I can see a bright future ahead. I think you'll make a splendid vet."

Hearing praise like that from such a well-qualified man made Leni's heart swell with pride.

"So, are you here for work?" she said, and then quickly added, "If you don't mind me asking."

"Indeed," replied Professor Flowers. "And my latest project is a most interesting one. It's quite unlike anything I've ever done before." He took out his hanky again and dabbed his forehead. "My co-workers back at the Institute are terribly excited. If it's successful, it's going to make history."

Leni was really intrigued now. What *could* he be here for?

"But I've only just arrived," he continued. "I don't really know my way around yet. And I need to sit down..."

"Why don't you rest out here on the front deck?" suggested Leni.

"Good idea," said Professor Flowers. On the deck there was a wicker table and two chairs. The old man eased himself slowly into one of them.

"Ah yes, that's better," said the professor. "There's a nice breeze out here. Come and join me and I'll tell you all about it."

Leni sat down on the other chair and Popcorn danced up and down in front of them.

She was all ears.

CHAPTER FOUR

Dead as a Dodo?

Over on the horizon, the glowing orange sun was beginning to sink, like a giant basketball with a puncture.

Professor Flowers stared out to sea. "I don't like flying, so I only travel by boat," he told Leni. "It's been a long journey getting here." He dabbed the top of his head again with his owl hanky. "I haven't got used to the climate yet though."

"You will," Leni assured him, noticing he'd rolled up his trouser legs. It wasn't even summer, either. This was July, which is wintertime in Mauritius.

Some herons were wading out in the bay. The ocean view seemed to soothe Professor Flowers. He crossed his

legs and began his story.

"I am here because of this island's most famous bird," he announced.

"You mean...the dodo?" asked Leni.

"Exactly," said the professor. "The dodo used to live in Mauritius...before it became extinct."

Leni nodded. She had grown up listening to tales of the legendary bird from "Muppa", as she called her grandmother. Muppa used to sit with Leni under the dodo tree and hold her spellbound for hours with her stories.

"The dodo was a big bird with tiny wings, a large, curved beak and plump rump with a flourish of tail feathers," said Professor Flowers.

He got up and started pacing up and down the deck. "It looked a bit like a giant pigeon, but it couldn't fly, so it waddled about, feasting on fruit and enjoying the sun. What a lifestyle! White sandy beaches and lush green jungle. Every day must have felt like a holiday for the lucky dodo."

"I know," Leni said. She'd heard the beginning many times. But she was all too aware of how the story ended — and it was not with a happily ever after.

"Mauritius used to be a desert island, full of plants and animals, but with no people living on it," the professor went on, as if he was lecturing to a room full of students. "The dodo had spent millions of years just being a dodo, doing what dodos do and minding its own dodo business. Then one day, humans came along."

"That's right," agreed Leni. "They—"

"And *that* certainly put a cat among the pigeons," said Professor Flowers, ignoring Leni and addressing his imaginary audience. "European sailors visited the island, and then the Dutch settled it in 1638. They discovered new species of animal they'd never seen before, including the dodo." He paused for a moment. "Imagine seeing a dodo for the first time!" he said. "It must have been quite a sight."

"Quite a sight," mimicked Popcorn. But the professor didn't seem to hear him either.

"Anyway, the sailors brought all manner of non-native animals along in their boats, and once pigs, dogs, rats and monkeys were running loose on the island, they soon got an appetite for dodo chicks — and eggs."

The professor sighed. "Up until then, the birds had enjoyed a life with no predators. They had their little wings, of course, but they didn't really need them, so they evolved out of flying. And instead of building nests up in trees, they built them on the ground. So their eggs were easy pickings for the hungry new animals. They were sitting ducks...or sitting dodos... You know what I mean." The professor waved his hand.

"The explorers ate dodo meat too," went on Leni.

"Oh, so you know all about it?" said Professor Flowers, as if suddenly realizing she was there.

"Yes," she replied. "My grandmother told me the whole story. Not everyone thought it tasted very nice, but in any case, the poor dodos didn't stand a chance. They say the last one died near the end of the seventeenth century."

Professor Flowers sat down again. "Yes," he said

sadly. "They were gone. Extinct. Wiped off the face of the planet for ever."

"Conservation wasn't even a thing then, not like it is now," said Leni.

"What?" said the professor. "Oh yes. There was no such thing as an endangered species in those days. If you could catch it, you could eat it. So those poor dodos didn't live happily ever after. They didn't even live *un*happily ever after. They didn't live at all."

They sat in silence for a moment, as if paying respect to the lost bird. Then Professor Flowers pointed a finger in the air. "But," he said, staring straight at Leni now. "What if we could change their fate? What if we could give dodos another chance at life? Just imagine that!"

Leni was baffled. "How?" she asked.

"I'm on the island because the bird science community is in a bit of a flutter right now," said the professor.

The pace of his voice quickened. "There have been lots of rumours recently that there are unexplored caves up in the highlands here. The buzz is that those caves could hold ancient dodo bones."

Leni wasn't sure what he was getting at. "Okay, but how would a bunch of old bones give dodos another chance at life?" she said.

"Because science has now advanced beyond our wildest dreams!" cried Professor Flowers. "Or perhaps I should say that science has caught up with our dreams. There is now a chance that we could bring long-lost species back to life."

He leaned forward and dropped his voice, as if someone else might hear. "I want to bring the dodo back from the dead."

"Really?" gasped Leni. "Can you actually make a dodo all over again?"

"Yes…well…maybe," said Professor Flowers, leaning back again in his chair. "There's a name for the science. It's called 'de-extinction'."

"So, like extinction, but in reverse?" asked Leni.

"Exactly," replied the professor. "It means bringing an extinct species back to life and I've developed my own special technique for doing it.

"There are lots of 'ifs' though," he continued. "*If* you

could find ancient dodo bones that had been preserved in good condition, *if* you could take them back to the lab and get some DNA out of a bone, and *if* it was in a good enough state, you *might* be able to use it to create a new dodo chick inside an egg. *If* the egg hatched into a healthy bird, we could see the world's first dodo in over three hundred years. Wouldn't that be amazing?"

"So amazing," breathed Leni.

"But before I even begin the process," cautioned the professor, "I'd need to find good quality dodo DNA."

"DNA, that's like, the building blocks of life," she said.

"That's right. And my mission hinges on finding it," said Professor Flowers. "We know that dodos only lived in one place in the world — here on Mauritius. Mauritius has lots of caves made out of old volcanoes and lava flows from past eruptions. If there were old dodo bones preserved in a lava cave and I could find them, I might be able to extract some ancient DNA from them."

"That's awesome," said Leni. "Is it hard to get the DNA out?"

27

"Well," replied the professor. "I'd need special equipment. And some help of course. And for that I'd call on…"

He hesitated for a moment and Leni held her breath.

She thought he was
going to say "you".

"A pigeon," he said.

"Oh," replied Leni flatly. "A pigeon?"

"A pigeon?" squawked Popcorn.

"Yes, a pigeon," said Professor Flowers. "Dodos were part of the pigeon family and nowadays pigeons are their closest living relatives." He wiped his glasses again with his hanky and put them back on. "It's quite tricky, but what I'd do is I'd reconstruct the dodo's DNA from the fragments of ancient DNA within the old bone, and put them together to make a genome — that's a complete set of instructions for a living thing."

Leni nodded.

"Then I'd take a pigeon cell, remove its original DNA and put the dodo DNA into the cell instead. Then I'd inject this new cell into an ordinary pigeon egg. Are you following?"

"I think so," said Leni slowly. "So it'd become a pigeon egg with a baby dodo growing inside it?"

"Correct," said the professor. "I'd ask a female and a male pigeon to play the parts of Mum and Dad. In nature, both pigeon parents take turns to sit on the egg to incubate it. Then if all went well, a dodo chick would hatch out. It's a long shot, but if it worked it would be extraordinary!" His eyes lit up like stars.

Leni couldn't believe her ears. "I just wish Muppa was here to hear this," she said to the professor.

"Muppa?"

"She's my grandmother, the one who told me all about dodos," Leni explained. "And she told me about other birds too. Birds that are still living in this country, that need our help to survive and not go extinct like the dodo. The pink pigeon, for instance. And the Mauritian kestrel…"

"And of course the echo parakeet, like our friend Popcorn here," added Professor Flowers.

"Exactly," said Leni. "Muppa opened my eyes to the world of birds and how important it is to look after them. But she's gone now. I miss her so much." Leni gazed into the distance, tears welling in her eyes.

"Oh I'm terribly sorry, I didn't want to upset you," said Professor Flowers kindly.

"That's okay," replied Leni.

She decided to change the subject. "So, are you

looking for any particular lava cave?" she asked.

Taking a long match, the professor lit the wick of a lantern so they could see better in the fading light. "As a matter of fact there *is* a cave that I'm interested in exploring," he answered. "But I haven't been able to find it on my map."

"What's it called?" asked Leni. "I might know where it is…"

"La Grotte de Vulcan," said the professor.

CHAPTER FIVE

A Rival's Arrival

"La Grotte de Vulcan? I know exactly where it is!" cried Leni. "It's a very remote cave, up in the highlands."

She would have said more, but at that moment they heard the sound of a vehicle approaching. It was another guest, Leni realized, one who'd just checked in and been given a key to their accommodation by her parents.

In the fading light, an open-topped jeep pulled up at the hut next to them. The headlights died as the driver switched off the engine. They heard the thud of heavy boots on sand and then saw the beam of a torch. The newcomer grabbed a large backpack from the passenger seat and walked up to the hut, numbered 603.

The new arrival didn't see them, and in the half-darkness, it was hard for them to make out a face properly. It was also partly obscured by a slouchy leather hat with a wide brim. But they could tell she was a woman. Professor Flowers peered through his glasses to try and get a better look. Then, all of a sudden, he let out a big groan.

"I don't believe it. It's *her*," he grumbled under his breath.

"Who?" asked Leni.

"Dratted ducks, why did *she* have to turn up?"

"Who? Why did who turn up?" asked Leni.

The woman unlocked her hut door and went inside, closing it behind her.

"Oh it's just…someone I didn't expect to see here," said Professor Flowers.

"Who is she?" persisted Leni.

"Who is she?" repeated Popcorn.

Professor Flowers sighed. "Her name is Professor Celia Scissorson. She's a rival of mine."

"Oh," said Leni. "So she's, like, another bird brain?"

"You could say that," replied Professor Flowers. "She's a professor at the Australian Avian Research Facility. She's a bit like me, but on the opposite side of the world. I should have known she'd have got wind of this lava cave rumour."

"You mean she's on the trail of the dodo too?"

"Without a doubt," said the professor grimly. "Like me, she is a scientist with a particular interest in birds. We both want to de-extinct the dodo...but that's about all we have in common."

Leni saw the lights go on inside the neighbouring hut.

"We're miles apart — not just literally, but also in our methods of working."

"So, you don't think much of her work?" asked Leni.

Professor Flowers paused to consider her question. "I wouldn't say that," he replied. "She's achieved many remarkable things. For instance, she made the world's first genetic copy of a kookaburra."

"Oh, I've heard of kookaburras," said Leni. "They live in Australia, don't they?"

"That's right. And she was the first to make a genetic

copy of one — a clone. But we have different ideas and methods," said Professor Flowers carefully. "What's more, she has taken a definite dislike to me.

"We've only met a few times, at conferences and the like," he continued, "but we have never seen eye to eye. And now she's here, she's going to be under my feet. Oh dear. That's shaken things up somewhat."

Leni thought for a moment. "You're both here for the same purpose," she said. "So why don't you work together on de-extincting the dodo?"

Professor Flowers looked at her as if she'd taken leave of her senses. "Are you cuckoo? Not on your life!" he barked. "Now we are both here, we will both want to be the *first* to de-extinct the dodo."

"Leni! Where are you? It's dinner time!" a voice called through the darkness.

"That's my dad," said Leni, getting up. "I'd better go."

"Better go!" shouted Popcorn.

Leni jumped off her seat and, taking Popcorn with her, disappeared home, leaving sandy footprints in her wake.

CHAPTER SIX

The Early Bird

Leni was so excited that dinner time, she could hardy eat. "Professor Flowers is from England, and he's trying to bring the dodo back to life," she told her mum and dad. "Imagine if he actually does it! The professor in number 603 is trying to do the same thing, only she's from Australia. I haven't met her yet though."

That night, Leni dreamed about a huge pigeon with a white moustache driving a jeep. It stopped on the beach, got out and laid an egg on the sand. The egg wobbled and little cracks started to appear. But just as it was about to hatch, she woke up to the sound of Popcorn squawking.

It was earlier than usual, but Leni bounced out of bed

and, over breakfast, carried on talking about the professors.

Her mother stroked her hair kindly. "Please don't bother the professors too much," she said. "They're here to do important research. Besides, you're on school holidays for three weeks and you've got lots of friends to play with."

Leni looked out towards the beach. White sand, blue sky. She could see it was going to be another perfect day, but she couldn't help thinking about the dodo that might soon waddle along that beach again. It wasn't even 7 a.m. yet, but Leni couldn't resist going back to the huts.

This time she found the other new guest, Professor Scissorson, outside number 603. She was middle-aged, tall and slim. She wore green safari shorts and a big brown hat, which bore the initials AARF and a kookaburra motif on the front. In the back seat of the jeep lay a couple of helmets with lights on the front and folded-up overalls. She'd laid out a large map on the bonnet and was studying it closely.

"Good morning," Leni said to the woman.

The new guest looked up. "Oh, g'day," she smiled back. "You're an early bird."

"I live here with my parents, who own the huts," she replied. "My name is Leni."

"Oh I see. Well I'm very pleased to meet you, Leni. My name's Professor Celia Scissorson," said the woman. "Hey, you might be able to help me actually," she went on. "I assume you know this area well?"

"Yes, pretty well," Leni answered.

"Sweet. You see, I'm working on an important project and I am looking for a cave." She smoothed out the map and started examining it again. "But I can't find it on here."

"Is it La Grotte de Vulcan, by any chance?" asked Leni.

Professor Scissorson looked up abruptly. "Yes it is!" she said. "How did you know?"

Before she could answer, the door of hut 187 opened and Professor Flowers stepped out. He was in his pyjamas. He yawned, stretched and took in the morning sunshine.

"Oh, hi, Professor Flowers!" Leni called out.

The English man turned towards her happy-sounding voice, but then stopped in his tracks at the sight of Professor Scissorson. As for the Australian, her jaw almost dropped to the ground when she saw who her new neighbour was.

"How on earth?" she began. "How did he…?"

But before she could say anything more, Leni piped up, "Professor Scissorson was just asking where La Grotte de Vulcan is!"

Professor Flowers snorted crossly and made a big deal of ignoring her by scratching his back and staring out towards the ocean.

"It's not marked on the map," Leni explained to Professor Scissorson. "And you can only get to it by one road. Actually, it's more of a dirt track. But your jeep will be able to handle it."

No one knew what to say next. "Right…no worries," said Professor Scissorson finally, although she actually looked pretty worried.

"No worries, no worries!" squawked Popcorn.

Professor Scissorson folded up her map and rummaged around in the back of the jeep. Leni could tell she was coming to terms with the shock of discovering that her arch rival was staying in the very next hut to her — and was probably after the same thing she was.

"Hey, I've got an idea," Leni chirped up. "You're both

looking for dodo bones and I know the territory. Why don't we all go together and I'll be your guide? It'll be fun!"

"Fun!" Popcorn repeated. "Fun!"

Professor Flowers started doodling in the sand with his big toe and Professor Scissorson began to readjust the straps on her backpack. Neither of them was rude enough to just come out and say, "No."

So Leni took it as a yes. "I'll just go and check it's okay with my mum and dad," she said. And before either professor could think of an excuse, she ran off, Popcorn flapping his wings behind her.

CHAPTER SEVEN

Dodo Heartland

Leni was so excited at the prospect of going on a cave-bound adventure that she was jumping around the room. "Please, Mum, can I take the professors to La Grotte de Vulcan — be their local guide? They're saying there could be ancient dodo bones in it, just waiting to be discovered."

"I don't know, Roshan," her mum said, looking at her dad with concern. "It's a rough track. That cave is so remote, and caves can be dangerous places..."

"Don't worry, the professors have lots of equipment," said Leni. "They've got caving gear, torches, everything we'll need. Professor Scissorson's going to drive us up there in her jeep. Can I go? Please? Dad?"

Her dad turned to her mum, "How about it, Manishi? She hasn't been this excited for ages. She's been down in the dumps since, you know…" His voice dropped and Leni knew it was because he was trying not to upset her. "Since we said goodbye to Muppa," he whispered to his wife. "It might be just what she needs…"

"Look," said her mum. "You can go —" Leni grinned and jumped up but her mother wasn't finished — "as long as you take the greatest care."

"Okay!" cried Leni. "I promise. Thanks, Mum and Dad!"

She dashed back to the huts. Professor Flowers had got dressed and was now standing awkwardly beside Professor Scissorson, who was dabbing sunscreen onto her nose.

"Come on, let's go!" cried Leni. She let herself into the front passenger side of the open-topped jeep and Popcorn perched on the sturdy frame.

The professors looked at each other. "After you," said Professor Scissorson through gritted teeth, indicating the back seat to Professor Flowers.

Professor Flowers clambered on board and then Professor Scissorson got in and started up the engine. Sand spat out behind the wheels in a brief flurry and they were away.

As they drove through the jungle, towards the highlands, Leni proudly pointed out the birds up in the foliage. Even just seeing a glimpse of a tail feather was enough for her to be able to identify a species.

The road headed on upwards, and soon became a dirt track. Valiantly, the jeep's chunky wheels clung on. Leni glanced round at Professor Flowers, who seemed shaken up by the bumpy ride.

"For pity's sake, slow down," he muttered, grabbing on to the door handle.

Professor Scissorson glared at Professor Flowers in her rear-view mirror.

"So, Leni," she said, "are you interested in dodos too?"

"Ye-e-e-e-s," Leni shouted back. The jeep was bouncing over potholes in the road, making her voice shake. "I love all birds. I want to be an avian

vet when I grow up."

Leni caught sight of a small lay-by ahead and asked Professor Scissorson to slow down. They paused at the roadside lookout. Dust hung in the air. But from this viewpoint, they could see the beautiful landscape spread out before them.

There was lush forest inland, and faraway in the distance, towards the ocean, they spotted fields of sugar cane.

"It's stunning," said Professor Scissorson, taking in the scene. "We're right in dodo heartland."

"I remember Muppa telling me how important it is to care for the natural world," said Leni. "That's my grandmother — Muppa. It's mainly because of her that I love the dodo and want to help you out. I just wish she could see me now...but she's gone." Leni looked off into the distance, the dust was getting into her eyes and they started to water.

"I'm sorry," said Professor Scissorson gently. "Did your grandmother pass away?"

Leni wiped her eyes with the back of her hand.

"No," she said. "She's gone to Australia. Your part of the world. She's staying with my uncle and aunt there."

"Oh," said Professor Scissorson.

"She's helping them out with their new baby," Leni went on. "My cousin. He's only a month old. It's the first time she's left the island." She blinked and scrunched up her face. "The dust is getting in my eyes, urgh!" she exclaimed.

"I bet she'll be thrilled to hear all your news," said Professor Scissorson. She put her foot on the accelerator and the jeep sped up again, taking them further up the dirt track.

"We've still got a way to go," said the professor. "I mean the science, not the road," she added. "We're only just getting to the point where de-extinction is even thinkable. I've worked with many other birds in my career, but I've dreamed of de-extincting a dodo from day one. And now I've developed my own technique for doing it. It's pretty revolutionary if I do say so myself."

Just then, they were interrupted by the sound of

snoring. Leni looked behind her. Somehow, Professor Flowers had fallen asleep in the back.

"Unbelievable," said Professor Scissorson, annoyed. "Keeping you up, were we?" she snorted.

"So what about him? What has he made?" asked Leni.

Professor Scissorson harrumphed. "He was the first person to clone a barn owl," she said.

"Oh yes, I've heard of that," Leni said brightly. "He took an owl's cell and grew an exact copy of the bird from it. I think they called it the Twit Two?"

"Between you and me, I think he did it more by accident than design," snapped Professor Scissorson. "He's absent-minded at the best of times. They say messiness is a sign of genius, but I'm not convinced..."

"He managed to get here, didn't he?" said Leni. "By land and boat as well."

"He certainly did," Professor Scissorson huffed.

Leni stared out into the skyline beyond, where the majestic volcano peaks kissed the sky. She couldn't see why Professor Scissorson was so bitter about Professor Flowers, he seemed perfectly nice to her.

"Anyway, we're here to find dodo bones," continued the Australian professor, gripping the steering wheel more firmly than ever. "I take it you know something of the dodo's sorry history?"

"I do," said Leni quietly. "We wiped them all out."

"Yes we did," said Professor Scissorson. "It's a crying shame. I love dodos — their chubby bodies, their curved beaks. I think they would've been adorable." Her eyes appeared to glaze over, like a pair of iced buns.

"They were totally trusting," added Leni.

"That's right," agreed the professor. "They were once thought of as clumsy and foolish, but I'll tell you what — we were the fools for wiping them out."

Leni sighed and nodded.

"But now, with a bit of scientific know-how, who knows?" said Professor Scissorson. "Perhaps we could give dodos another chance."

"Another chance!" repeated Popcorn. His squawk woke Professor Flowers from his slumber.

"Uh? Are we there yet?" mumbled the old man.

CHAPTER EIGHT

La Grotte de Vulcan

Professor Flowers woke up from his back-seat slumber in the nick of time, because just then they rounded a corner in the road and Leni cried, "Stop!"

Professor Scissorson slammed on the brakes. "Here we are. La Grotte de Vulcan!" announced Leni.

"La Grotte de Vulcan!" repeated Popcorn, sounding like a train station announcer.

Leni was relieved the bumpy ride had come to an end and they were on firm ground again. Professor Flowers got out of the jeep and Leni noticed Professor Scissorson slammed the door harder than she needed to. "You're welcome," she muttered.

49

Now they were high up in the highlands, the temperature had dropped. Leni breathed in the cooler air. All was silent, except for the sound of rocks crunching underneath their boots and the calls of distant birds in the jungle below.

The adults both started to put on zip-fronted overalls. "Here you are," said Professor Scissorson, throwing Leni a green suit from the back of her jeep. "It'll protect you inside the cave." The all-in-one suit was so big, she had to roll up the sleeves and trouser legs.

Professor Scissorson swapped her slouchy "bush hat", as she called it, for a caver's helmet with a light on the front. "Put this on," she said, handing a similar white helmet to Leni. Professor Flowers had his own helmet with the IBBB logo on it. He took out a small torch and duct-taped it to the front. "Perfect," he said to himself.

Leni led the two professors to the entrance of the cave. It was very dark; they couldn't see more than a few metres inside.

Just as they were about to go in, Leni felt someone grabbing her sleeve. It was Professor Flowers.

"Stop," he whispered urgently.

"What is it?" she replied.

"Did you hear that?" whispered the professor. His eyes darted around.

"Hear what?" said Professor Scissorson loudly.

"Ssssh," whispered the old man. For a while they stood listening. Leni looked around but couldn't see anything out of the ordinary.

"I don't know," said Professor Flowers eventually. "I thought I heard a voice. Maybe I was mistaken." He hauled on his canvas backpack.

"Let's go inside," said Professor Scissorson. She'd fastened a belt over her overalls, from which hung a compass and a roll of white tape.

Leni had been here before, but still, there was something exciting about this cave, and so she took a deep breath and stepped into the darkness. Guided only by helmet-torch beams, criss-crossing as they searched for clues, she could make out the gnarled, grooved sides and roof of the lava cave. She carefully picked her way over boulders and stones.

"Oops," she gasped, slipping on some moss.

Professor Flowers also lost his footing slightly. "Suffering seagulls!" he shouted, his voice echoing in the hollow cave.

"Are you okay?" called Leni. She turned and her beam picked out the figure of the old man scrambling over the rock just behind her.

"Yes, I think so," he replied. "I fell over and hurt my backside. This cooled lava is rough stuff."

Leni felt Popcorn digging his claws into her shoulder. Professor Flowers was right behind and Professor Scissorson edged along at the back, hugging the wall. The light from their head torches illuminated the hardened dark lava of the cave's inner walls, arching over them.

The daylight at the tunnel's entrance faded behind them as they went deeper and deeper into the cave. The torchlight picked out strange lava formations hanging from above, like stalactites made out of melted chocolate.

The three of them searched for what seemed like hours, but they couldn't find anything. *Can there really be any dodo bones here?* wondered Leni. No bones would mean no dodo. She didn't want to confess it to the professors, but she was beginning to lose hope.

The two adults were still looking high and low and each was blaming the other for their lack of success. "Why's she in such a hurry?" grumbled Professor Flowers to Leni. "We might miss something important."

"That dilly-dallyer has slowed us all down," muttered Professor Scissorson, thinking only Leni could hear her. But Popcorn repeated "Dilly-dallyer!" and the sound resonated in the hollow cave.

Just then, something hit Professor Scissorson squarely in the face. "Argh, what was that?" she shrieked. It felt like a wing, but this was no bird. Suddenly a whole army of the flying animals flapped past them, almost sweeping Popcorn away as they did so.

"Don't panic!" shouted Professor Flowers. "Just keep still."

"Bats," said Leni when the commotion had died down. "Don't worry, Professor Scissorson, they're harmless. We must have disturbed them, that's all."

Now they found themselves staring at a large, shallow crater in the middle of the cave floor. It looked like a giant chocolate muffin that had collapsed on the top.

"This is a lava pond," said Leni. Just as she went to move around the crater, the light of her helmet torch illuminated something curious. Something small and greyish. It was lying wedged between two boulders within the shallow crater. It was jagged, and didn't look much like anything. But something told her she should check it out.

Cautiously, Leni ventured over to get a closer look. Using the light of the torch, she could make out that it was about the length of a pencil and a couple of centimetres wide.

"Come here, both of you," she whispered urgently. The professors moved towards her and their torch beams converged on the long thin object. "What's that?"

"Well, blow me down with a goose feather," said Professor Flowers, whistling through his teeth.

"You beauty," whispered Professor Scissorson, marvelling at the object.

"Do you think it's a dodo bone?" asked Leni softly.

"It's hard to tell in this light, but I'd say it looks very much like the tibiotarsus bone of an adult *Raphus cucullatus*," said Professor Flowers. "Would you agree, Professor Scissorson?"

"I would, Professor," she agreed gravely.

"Um, what's a Raphus cuckoo-whatever-it-was?" asked Leni.

"I'm sorry, I mean yes, it's a dodo bone," explained Professor Flowers. "Well done, eagle-eyed Leni!" He smiled.

Leni was mesmerized. She picked up the bone in her hand.

"Careful," warned Professor Flowers. "It's a leg bone. It is very, *very* delicate."

"It's perfect!" breathed Professor Scissorson in awe.

Leni could feel the pressure on both sides, as if the cave walls were slowly closing in on her. She knew she had something that both professors wanted desperately. Now, in the torchlit grotto, she found herself in the middle of a battle for the bone.

"Remember, Leni, I drove us up to the cave, so the bone should really be mine," Professor Scissorson said in her sweetest voice. "Fair's fair."

"Hang on a minute. I was the first person to tell you all about it," argued Professor Flowers. "I deserve the bone." He looked at her like a dog who'd lost his favourite toy.

Leni gripped the tibiotarsus tightly. They both wanted

it so much, but did either one of them deserve it more than the other? It was an impossible choice. She glanced over at Popcorn, who was sitting on a nearby rock. "Who should have the bone, Professor Scissorson or Professor Flowers?" she asked the bird.

"Professor Scissorson," replied Popcorn. Professor Scissorson smiled, self-satisfied, and grasped the bone by one end.

Leni let go, but Popcorn hadn't finished his sentence yet. "Or Professor Flowers," he squawked.

Quick as a flash the old man grabbed the other end of the bone. Suddenly they'd lost their cool and were squabbling over it like two young children. Leni looked on helplessly.

"Give it to me," growled Professor Scissorson.

"Never!" he shot back. "It's my bone!"

"Let go!" she continued, hoping the older man's strength would desert him. "Let go of it now!"

"Over my dead body," grunted Professor Flowers.

In their desperate tug of war, any concerns for handling the bone with care were forgotten and Leni was terrified it would break right there in front of them.

Then, all of a sudden, Professor Flowers lost his grip on the bone slightly and slipped backwards. Professor Scissorson, knocked off balance with the sudden release in tension, lost her grip too. The precious tibiotarsus soared up and sailed off into the darkness.

There was a stunned silence, which Professor Scissorson finally broke as she got to her feet. "Oh great," she said sarcastically. "Now where has it gone?"

"It wasn't my fault, you let go first," protested Professor Flowers.

"I did not," fumed Professor Scissorson.

"Yes you did."

"I did not."

"Did so."

"Did not."

"Professors, please!" interrupted Leni. "This isn't helping. Let's calm down. It can't be far away." She looked around. They were at a slight bend in the tunnel and so, guiding herself with the beam of her helmet torch, she slowly edged round the craggy corner.

What she saw on the other side made Leni blink in disbelief. Her torch beam illuminated more bones. There were dozens of them, hundreds probably, scattered around like feathers after a pillow fight. They lay wedged in the hardened lava ridges, or stuck higgledy-piggledy between boulders. Wings, feet, legs. Bones, upon bones, upon bones.

Could these all be precious dodo bones? Leni's head swam with questions. If they were, how had this graveyard ended up here? Had the dodos all taken shelter here before the lava from a freak volcanic eruption had claimed them in its scalding grip? Or had the poor dodos perhaps fallen prey to hungry sailors who'd had a big feast and dumped the bones here centuries ago?

Leni was bamboozled. The poor dodos, she thought. They'd had such bad luck. And now they were piled up here, all forgotten. Until now.

CHAPTER NINE

A Bone to Pick

The professors' mouths gaped open like a pair of hungry hatchlings. They could hardly believe that lying there, right in front of them, were hundreds of dodo bones.

Leni was bewildered too, but the sound of a zip being pulled snapped her back into the moment.

Professor Scissorson opened her backpack and got out a clear, resealable plastic bag. Then she produced something which resembled a rolled-up napkin and unfurled it on the cave floor to reveal lots of small tools, all neatly lined up.

"I think I'll have a leg bone. Hang on, there's a nice-looking femur," she said. "Excuse me, Leni, if I could just reach over…there we go. Sweet."

She grasped the delicate bone with a pair of tweezers and dropped it into the plastic bag as if it was a piece of evidence at a crime scene.

"Well, well, well, what's this?" said Professor Flowers. He picked up a thin bone with a pair of what appeared to be salad tongs. "Hmm, that's a funny-looking bone."

Then he realized what it was. "Ah, it's an upper arm bone — a humerus," he said.

"Maybe that's why it looks funny," said Professor Scissorson, and giggled.

It was the first time Leni had heard her laugh.

Leni helped both professors pick out a few bones each and, in the torchlight, they gazed at them in wonder.

"What a find," whispered Professor Scissorson gleefully.

"It's hard to tell, but they look in good condition," said Professor Flowers, who'd laid out his specimens on his hanky. "We'll have to examine them more closely in the lab to know for sure."

"Let's get back now," said Professor Scissorson, "while the going's good."

But as they packed away, Professor Flowers started to get anxious. "Oh, blithering bullfinches," he muttered. "I'm not sure I can remember which way we came…"

"Don't worry, Professor, I marked the walls with white tape. We can just follow it back. It's quite straightforward," said Professor Scissorson a little smugly.

"Quite straightforward," echoed Popcorn.

There were many tunnels branching off the main one and a wrong turn could have left them lost inside the labyrinth of lava. They followed the white tape markers for nearly an hour. Leni was getting hungry and wished the dripping, cooled lava formations really *were* made of chocolate. But they finally got to the cave entrance, and Leni was glad to feel the warm sunshine on her face as they emerged into the outside world again.

Professor Flowers blinked in the light, removed his helmet and ran his hand though his wispy hair. "Thank you, Leni," he said.

"Yes, thank you so much," added Professor Scissorson, patting her backpack with its precious cargo inside. "This is a major breakthrough. You've done us – I mean me – a great service."

Professor Flowers had all the energy of a young man. "If these bones contain DNA, and it is in good enough condition, who knows? We could use it to create a real dodo again. Just think! The dodo redone!" he cried.

"We mustn't get ahead of ourselves. It's…it's unprofessional," said Professor Scissorson sniffily.

But it was clear to Leni that it was hard for either of them to contain their excitement. They threw their overalls and helmets in the back of the jeep and hopped in.

This time though, Popcorn didn't join them. He took off and disappeared into the jungle. He sometimes did that. Leni knew he'd catch up with them again later.

"I can't wait to get home and tell my mum and dad what we've found," said Leni. She grinned as she climbed into the passenger seat.

"To Baie de la Vie, on the double, and put your foot down, Professor Scissorson!" shouted Professor Flowers.

For a brief moment, it was as if their rivalry was forgotten. Maybe it was just a short-term truce, but with some dodo bones each, both the professors were boosted with hope and Leni felt glad.

The jeep sped off in a cloud of dust with a giddy Professsor Scissorson at the wheel. They practically glided over the potholes that marked the road, with dreams of dodos dancing through their heads.

But Professor Flowers hadn't been mistaken when he thought he heard something earlier at the cave entrance. And what none of them saw as they drove off, were the two stocky figures standing on a large rock, their menacing forms silhouetted against the sun.

CHAPTER TEN

A Sweet Tooth

Making his way home, Popcorn soared over the jungle treetops and down towards the ocean. Before long, he got a bird's-eye view of the acres and acres of sugar cane growing in the fields below him.

At the centre of one of the biggest sugar plantations stood an enormous mansion surrounded by neat, well-tended gardens. It had a vast, flat-roofed front porch, white pillars and shuttered dormer windows.

Popcorn flew over a statue of the mansion's bald-headed owner, which stood on the sweeping front drive, smiling as if to welcome visitors.

The owner of this magnificent estate was a sugar

tycoon called Benny Shoober, and he was the richest man on the island. Most people knew him as the Sugar King of Mauritius. This was because of the successful sugar empire he had built up after coming to the island from South Africa.

Right now, Benny Shoober was leaning against the mantelpiece in his lavishly decorated office. A Hawaiian shirt strained at the buttonholes across his belly and his bald head shone slightly with a coating of afternoon sweat. He was looking at his wife, who was wearing a leopard-print swimsuit and staring into the mirror over the mantelpiece.

"Oh, Benny, honey," she said in a voice that was sweet and yet scratchy at the same time. "Do my lips look crinkly around the edges?"

Giavanna, or Mrs Shoober III, was fond of wearing large, gold-hooped earrings, lashings of perfume and a thick mask of make-up. She was obsessed with looking young and had tried every anti-ageing cream, balm, ointment and serum on the market in an attempt to turn back the clock on her appearance. No one knew quite how old she was, and nobody dared ask.

"I've been trying a new lip ointment for three weeks now and I can't see any difference, honey," Giavanna complained to her husband.

"Sweetlips, your mouth looks perfect," Benny tried to reassure her. He took a sticky bun from a silver platter on the coffee table in front of him. His fingers were chubby and bore several chunky gold rings.

"C'mon, give me a kiss," he said, puckering up.

Giavanna turned towards him and planted a big smacker on his mouth.

"You look stunning, sweetlips," said Benny. He took a big bite from the bun.

"But I don't look any younger…" said Giavanna glumly. She turned back to the mirror.

"What's the ointment made of, anyway?" asked Benny.

"Camel saliva," replied his wife.

Benny almost spat out his mouthful of bun.

Giavanna looked longingly at the plate of pastries. Benny swallowed and then said, "Go on, treat yourself."

"Benny!" she snorted.

"What?" he asked.

"You don't get it, do you, honey?" she said scratchily. "A pastry is full of sugar! Think about it!"

And that's what makes it so delicious, thought the tycoon. But there was no pleasing some people.

Giavanna wrapped a leopard-print robe around herself. "I'm off for a swim," she rasped. "See you later."

Oh well, thought Benny, *all the more for me*. He went to reach for another bun and almost knocked one of his prized trophies off the mantelpiece with his elbow. "Oops," he mumbled, just managing to stop it before it toppled over. He stood it back up and smirked. He was remembering the moment he went up to collect that trophy, the award for "Best Sugar Cubes" at the annual Sugar Makers Movers and Shakers Gala last year.

Instead of another bun, Benny decided to take a cigar from a gold-plated case. It was even chunkier than his fingers. He lit it, a plume of smoke rose up and the ceiling fan swirled it around the room.

He caught sight of his reflection in the mirror over the mantelpiece. He cleared his throat and flashed a smile, revealing his yellowing teeth.

"With Shoober, life is sweet," he said to his own reflection. "Life is Sweet" was the slogan for his sugar brand and it was on all of the sugar products which came out of his factory. Whenever an advert for Shoober Sugar was on the TV or radio, the slogan came with it.

"Hi boss," came a gruff voice behind him. Shoober jumped, coughed and spilled cigar ash on his shirt. "Oh it's you," he said, irritated at being interrupted. He brushed the ash away and stubbed out the cigar in an ashtray. "Don't you know how to knock, Pawpaw?"

"I did, but you didn't hear, boss," replied the man. "Sorry, but we need to talk to you urgently."

Pawpaw was tall and his high forehead was crowned with black slicked-back hair. His eyes were sunken-in and his squarish chin had a little dimple in the middle. His hands were like baseball mitts and on his knuckles were tattooed the words "love" and "hate".

"Yeah, something came up," added a much shorter man standing next to him. This was his sidekick, Beanbag. He had shiny shoes, short hair, rosy cheeks and was keen to please.

"We just saw something you might find interesting," said Pawpaw.

"Yeah, some new arrivals on the island," added Beanbag.

"A man and a woman," went on Pawpaw.

"So far, so what?" said Shoober. "Gimme the bullet points." He sat down on the velvet couch.

"They're both scientists," said Beanbag.

"And they are on the island because they are trying to bring back the dodo," declared Pawpaw.

"Bring it back? From where?" asked their boss.

Pawpaw cleared his throat. "From the dead."

CHAPTER ELEVEN

De-Eggs-Stink-Shun

Benny Shoober sat bolt upright on his velvet couch. Scientists bringing back the dodo? From the dead? This really was news.

"Are you sure?" he asked.

"Sure as eggs is eggs," said Beanbag. "We got a tip-off and followed them to La Grotte de Vulcan today. They were in the cave, snooping around for dodo bones."

Shoober snorted. "But why? What good would old bones be?" he asked.

"They said they can get some Ds and As out of them," said Beanbag, catching sight of himself in the mirror and smoothing down his hair. "Whatever they are."

"DNA, dimwit!" corrected Pawpaw. "They reckon if they can get some old DNA out of the bones, they can make a new dodo out of it," he explained to Shoober. "It's called de-eggs-stink-shun," he added.

"They're planning to put the DNA into a pigeon egg, and then they think the egg will hatch into a dodo chick."

"There's a girl with them too. And a parrot," said Beanbag.

"Hmm..." Shoober got up and started pacing the room, rubbing his chin with his left hand. "This is not good news," he said.

He stopped to look at the map on his office wall behind his desk. It showed the mansion and the surrounding fields, and an area to the west marked out in red stripes. There was another area to the north that was marked out in the red stripes too. At least, it had been before someone put big black crosses over it.

"Look what happened here," he said to the two men, pointing to the area which now resembled a cemetery. "I wanted to expand my wonderful empire by turning this land into more sugar-cane fields.

"But I was stopped at the last minute."

"By who?" asked Beanbag.

"Eco-warriors," said Shoober sourly. "You know, those silly do-gooders who think they're saving the planet."

Pawpaw nodded.

"They went on about the so-called Mauritius kestrel losing its habitat if I turned that forest into cane fields," Shoober scoffed. "They protested. They organized demonstrations. They waved banners around. And they blocked me from getting that land."

"Party poopers," muttered Pawpaw.

"This area," said Shoober, walking back to the map, "I wanted to buy up too. But those crazy tree-huggers interfered and claimed it was the echo parakeet's territory. And again, they got their way. Somehow." He picked up a black marker pen and began scoring big black crosses through that area as well.

The Sugar King snapped the lid back on his pen and pointed it at the men. "But this time," he vowed, "they are not going to get away with it!"

He swapped the black pen for a red one and started marking out a new area in the west with scarlet stripes. "This is the area I've set my sights on," he said. "It's jungle at the moment, but if I buy it, I'll chop down those annoying trees and turn it into fields of sugar cane." He treated them to another view of his unlovely gnashers.

His mood then darkened once again. "But if dodos come back, they'll ruin everything!" he blasted. He banged his big chunky-ringed fist on the oak desk so hard it shook.

"Yes, boss," said Beanbag nervously.

"With dodos back on the scene, those eco-warriors will stop me once again!" ranted Shoober. "They'll claim this land is 'dodo heartland' or some other nonsense. But that territory should be mine! For sugar! More sweet, sugary, Shoober Sugar!"

"We hear you, boss," Beanbag gulped.

"They think they can just come here and make dodos and then set them free to run riot, do they? Well, I've got news for them: dodos are extinct, and extinct they need to stay!"

"Pesky dodos!" growled Pawpaw.

"Exactly!" agreed Shoober. "They're nothing but clumsy, overgrown pigeons! Giant rats with wings! I cannot let them invade the island and hijack my precious land."

All of a sudden, Shoober stopped in his tracks. An egg-shaped idea was starting to form in his egg-shaped head.

He turned back to the two henchmen. "I want you to watch these professors like hawks," he told them slowly. "And if they make a dodo egg, I want you to steal it and bring it to me. Understand?"

Then he dropped his voice to a hush, walked over to the coffee table and took another bun in his hand — a cream bun this time. "I want to make sure that any dodo is re-extincted before it

is even de-extincted." He squeezed the bun so hard the cream burst out onto the floor.

"Okay, boss," Beanbag said.

"Those bird-loving loons will not stop me this time! Because there will be no dodo. No dodo at all!" he thundered.

The men stood in silence before him.

"Well, what are you waiting for? Get to it!" he barked.

The pair beat a hasty retreat and Shoober licked the cream off his hand. He turned back to the mirror. "With Shoober, life is sweet," he cooed to himself.

"Life is sweet! Life is sweet!" Sitting on the window ledge was Popcorn, and he was enjoying mimicking the tycoon.

But Shoober was in no mood for this. He darted over to the window. "Dratted bird!" he shouted. "Get out of here!"

"Life is sweet! Life is sweet!" repeated Popcorn in an identical South African accent. He hopped merrily from foot to foot.

"Off you go!" snapped Shoober. "Echo parakeets, you're nothing but a menace! Go away! Get lost!"

He shooed Popcorn away from the window and scanned the rows of sugar cane stretching out in the fields below.

"One day there will be sugar-cane fields as far as the eye can see!" he vowed. "Nobody is going to stop me expanding my empire! Not kestrels, not parakeets and certainly not dastardly DODOS!"

CHAPTER TWELVE
An Outing

The next morning, the sun slowly appeared on the eastern horizon like a basketball being pumped up, and by 7 a.m. Leni was over at the huts to see if anyone was about yet.

Professor Scissorson's shutters were still closed but she found Professor Flowers already dressed and about to head off into the nearest town on a bike he'd hired. "Would you like to accompany me, young Leni?" he asked her. "I brought over some equipment from England in my trunk, but there are a few more bits and bobs I need before I begin work. I want to get a head start and all that —" he nodded towards Professor Scissorson's hut and whispered — "before *she* gets up."

Popcorn perched on the handlebars of Leni's bike and came along for the ride as the two of them cycled into town. Arriving at the local bazaar, Leni wondered what the old man would make of all the noise and bustle.

Luckily, he loved it. There seemed to be dodos everywhere — weaved into basketwork bags, popping up on pairs of slippers, appearing on baseball caps, mugs and key rings.

"For an extinct animal, it strikes me that here at least, the dodo is very much alive," remarked the professor. "Look, dodo snow globes, dodo bathrobes, dodo yo-yos..."

They passed a clothing stall. "Do you want to get some shorts?" asked Leni, pointing at his rolled-up trouser legs.

"Good idea," replied the professor.

"Good idea!" repeated Popcorn.

With the help of the salesman, the old man picked out a pair and went to try them on.

"What do you think?" he said, stepping out from behind the changing room curtain and doing a twirl.

"They suit you..." said Leni.

"Down to the ground?" asked Professor Flowers.

"Well, down to the knees at least," said Leni.

"Good," said the professor. "I'll just keep them on, then," he told the salesman.

Next, he purchased a bottle of sunscreen, and from there they went on looking for the "bits and bobs" the professor was after.

They came to a stand full of kitchenware, and Leni showed him a Mauritian pestle and mortar — a "*roche cari*" and "*baba*". The "*roche cari*", or "curry rock", was a grey, grooved slab made of volcanic rock, with a matching, heavy-duty pin (the "*baba*").

"How much?" Professor Flowers asked the salesman.

"One thousand five hundred rupees," replied the man. The professor got out his wallet to pay. But Popcorn, who was perched on an upturned cooking pot, chimed in.

"One thousand five hundred rupees?" he squawked, sounding as if he couldn't believe it.

"Okay, okay. One thousand three hundred," said the seller.

"One thousand three hundred?" screeched Popcorn. Leni wondered if he was going to add, "*You've got to be joking!*" and stifled a laugh.

But the seller seemed to enjoy the game. He went down to one thousand two hundred.

"One thousand two hundred?" shrieked Popcorn as if he had never been so insulted. By now, the haggling pair had collected a small crowd of onlookers.

"One thousand rupees," declared the salesman. "My final price."

"Final price!" squawked Popcorn, and that settled it. Professor Flowers paid the salesman, who then began to wrap up the *roche cari* and *baba* with some old pages of the newspaper, the *Mauritian Pigeon Post*.

"He drives a hard bargain," said Leni, smiling at the professor and stroking Popcorn's feathers.

The professor rubbed his hands together. "I can't wait to set it all up and get to work," he said.

All of a sudden, the sound of Benny Shoober's voice came over a nearby radio. "Life is sweet," rang out the jingle.

"Life is sweet! Life is sweet!" squawked Popcorn.

"What's he saying?" said Professor Flowers.

"Oh, it's just an advert on the radio. For sugar," explained Leni. "Popcorn's copying the catchphrase."

Professor Flowers listened. "With Shoober Sugar, life is sweet," came Shoober's gravelly voice over the airwaves. Leni shuddered.

"Urgh, I don't like that man," she said.

"Who?" asked Professor Flowers.

"It's Benny Shoober. He's the Sugar King of Mauritius. He is always trying to buy up land so he can chop down trees and grow more sugar. He wants to take away the habitat of some of the rarest birds in Mauritius. He's the richest — and greediest — man on the island. Even his voice gives me the creeps."

Professor Flowers frowned. "He doesn't sound like

my sort of person," he remarked. "Anyhow, I am rather hungry. Do you know somewhere we could have a bite to eat?"

"Yes," replied Leni. "Do you like split peas?"

"I certainly do." Professor Flowers patted his tummy.

"Follow me, then," said Leni.

The professor stuffed his purchase into his bag and they walked out onto the street. The smell coming from a nearby food cart was too good to resist.

Leni ordered two portions of something wrapped in greaseproof paper, and passed one to Professor Flowers.

"What is this — a pancake?" he asked, peering inside the paper.

"It's *d'holl puri*," said Leni. "It's a type of Mauritian bread, made with split peas. And there's butter-bean curry inside it."

Professor Flowers tucked in. "Mmm, it's delicious," he said between mouthfuls.

They ate while enjoying the bustle of street life, until at last the professor wiped remnants of curry from his moustache with his hanky. "Now how about seconds?"

CHAPTER THIRTEEN

Shipments of Equipment

After their trip to the market, Leni and Professor Flowers cycled back to the huts while Popcorn flew back to the bay by himself. By the time the cyclists arrived they were both sweating and caked in a thin layer of dust.

Leni noticed a big van pulling up outside hut 603. Professor Scissorson popped her head out of her front door. "My lab equipment!" she said happily. The delivery men unloaded box after box of hefty-looking kit with "Fragile" and "This Way Up" stickers all over it.

"Over here, guys," she called out to the two baseball-capped men. "That's a big one. Thanks, mate." Then, from under the brim of her hat, she caught sight of Leni and Professor Flowers.

"Oh, g'day," she said curtly, as if her day had just become a little less good.

"G'day!" squawked Popcorn, who'd just landed on Leni's bike handlebars again.

"What's happening?" asked Leni. "You look as though you're moving in for good."

"No, no, it's just some of my equipment from home," said Professor Scissorson. "I had it shipped over."

She signed for her deliveries and then turned to the dusty duo.

"So where have you two been this morning?" she asked them.

"Into town," replied Leni. She looked at Professor Flowers, holding his bag containing the *roche cari*, sunscreen, and a few dodo snow globes he'd bought at the last minute. He didn't have nearly as much equipment as Professor Scissorson by the looks of it.

"My gene machine should be arriving any time now," said Professor Flowers casually.

Leni wondered what he was talking about. A gene machine? What was that? The air felt warm and Leni sensed an awkwardness hanging in it. Popcorn scratched the back of his head with his left claw. Before long, a very strong smell cut through the awkwardness. Professor Scissorson wrinkled up her nose in disgust.

"Who did that?" she complained.

Leni turned to the likely culprit, but he was already heading towards hut 187. "All the gear but no idea," she heard him mutter under his breath as he disappeared inside.

"That's revolting," said Professor Scissorson, wafting the air with her hand.

"That's revolting!" repeated Popcorn.

Just then, a motorcycle driver pulled up with a big box strapped to the back. "Delivery for Professor Showers!" he announced.

The box was plastered with stamps. *It must be his gene machine*, thought Leni, *whatever that is*. She took it from the driver.

"Professor Flowers!" she called. "A delivery for you!"

"Just leave it on the deck, thanks," called a muffled voice from inside. "I'll be there in a jiffy."

Leni put down the box and then Professor Scissorson called out to her. "Would you mind giving me a hand?" she asked. "I could do with some help unpacking."

Why not? thought Leni. She'd already helped Professor Flowers plenty that day and there was a lot of stuff for Professor Scissorson to unload. And she was curious. What could be inside all the boxes?

She was about to go next door when she thought she saw something moving in the bushes. She looked over. Was it Popcorn? No, he was on the beach outside Professor Scissorson's hut, tucking into half a banana which one of the delivery men had given to him. She looked over at the bushes again. Nothing. Oh well, she decided, it must've been her imagination.

Inside hut 603, Professor Scissorson was busy unwrapping her items. There were bottles and dishes, flasks and masks, all encased in bubble wrap. "Maybe I'm fussy, but I like to have my favourite apparatus, even when I'm working out in the field," she said.

Leni began to unwrap a cube-shaped machine with a pop-up lid. She pressed the button, and the lid opened to reveal twelve little holes in a circle.

"What's this?" asked Leni.

"A centrifuge," replied Professor Scissorson. "It's a critical piece of kit. It spins round at a very high speed, so fast that it can separate different substances from each other. After I take out the DNA from the dodo bone, I plan to spin it in this little beauty."

"Oh," said Leni, pressing the lid back down.

"I don't know about you, but I've never heard of a gene machine before," said the professor. "I use one of these — a DNA reader." She produced a slim black object the size of a mobile phone and plugged it into her laptop.

Then she lowered her voice. "Between you and me," she said, "I think anything Professor Flowers has created has been more accidental than deliberate."

"Like the barn owl?" said Leni.

"Yes," said Professor Scissorson. "It was quite a feat but I don't know how he managed it. Honestly, I don't think he has much of an idea what he's doing."

"Maybe he'd appreciate a bit of help," suggested Leni.

"Perhaps. Or maybe he'd be better off leaving it to me.

I would have thought he'd prefer to relax in a deckchair with his paper instead of chasing around after dodo bones."

"But he's so enthusiastic," began Leni. "And he has years of experience…"

"Hmm," considered Professor Scissorson. "Sure, he's had some successes. People were wowed by his barn owl clone — the Twit Two. But my cloned kookaburra was just as impressive. The original was a male and I created a genetic copy. They called it the Kooka-brother."

"Oh, yes," said Leni, "Professor Flowers told me about it."

"But he stole my thunder," said Professor Scissorson, unable to hide her bitterness. She started popping some bubble wrap in frustration.

Leni peered out of the window towards Professor Flowers's hut. There he was on the front deck, bending down slowly to pick up his parcel.

"This time, though, it will be different," vowed Professor Scissorson. She unzipped a large bag and Leni saw her pull out a white plastic coverall. "I need to wear this protective suit. And these," she added, waving a pair of blue rubber lab gloves.

"Why? Is dodo DNA dangerous?" asked Leni.

"Not to us. It's actually humans who are dangerous to the DNA," said the professor. "I wear this so I don't taint the dodo DNA with my own."

Next, she brought out a large helmet. "You can't be too careful," she said, polishing the visor with a special wipe from a tub.

"So, now you've got all your gear, what's next?" asked Leni.

"Next up," replied Professor Scissorson, flexing her hands, "is finding some parents for our dodo-to-be."

CHAPTER FOURTEEN

Homes to Roost

Before breakfast the next morning, Leni and Popcorn went to see what was new with the professors. The sounds of banging and sawing greeted them as they drew closer to the huts.

The source of the noise was Professor Flowers. He was holding a hammer and banging nails one by one into a rickety wooden storage unit. The about-to-be-hammered nails were pinched between his lips, which made it difficult for Leni to work out what he was saying.

"'Erro, m' fludgling," he greeted her.

"Pardon?" said Leni.

"Pardon?" chorused Popcorn.

Professor Flowers spat the nails into his palm. "Hello, my fledgling!" He laughed. "Just making a loft for my pigeons."

"Oh, right," she replied.

"I'm cobbling it together from some old broken book cases and storage units," he explained.

"Where did you get them?"

"I was taking a stroll and came across a man loading the old bookshelves into the back of a van, ready to take to the tip," said the professor. "I told him I'd be happy to give them a new home. So he brought them here for me instead! What a stroke of luck, eh?"

Leni wondered about that. The loft did look pretty rickety, but at least the professor had a positive attitude to recycling.

He was breaking into a sweat from the effort. "I just need to make a few finishing touches and my pigeon hotel will be ready," he beamed. After some more hammering, Professor Flowers tested it to see if it would stand up on its own in the sand. It did — but only just. It looked like it might topple over at any moment.

"Now I just need some residents," said the professor. He pulled out a bag of grain from his pocket. "It shouldn't take long to attract some with this," he said. "This stuff is like gold dust. It never fails."

Leni looked at the label. It read "Economy Pigeon Seed".

"They'll be here before you can say 'Nelson's Column'," he assured her.

Professor Flowers sprinkled some of the seed mix on the ground. Sure enough, it didn't take long for a flock of pigeons to fly down and start pecking away. A couple of the bolder ones sat on his shoulders and one even perched on top of his head.

"Oi, cheeky chap!" laughed the old man, his wispy eyebrows shooting up in surprise.

"Now," he continued, trying to move the bird off his head, "I'm going to show you something. How to tell the males and females apart."

"Okay," replied Leni.

"The main thing to remember is that the males act in a specific way," said Professor Flowers. He proceeded to puff out his chest, waggle his elbows and strut around in a circle. "Like this."

Leni laughed.

"Males strut about, they like to show off," he explained. "But females don't."

Popcorn was keeping his distance — in fact he'd flown off to the tree house. But someone else was just arriving. Leni heard the unmistakable sound of Professor Scissorson's jeep approaching.

The professor slowed down and parked in front of her hut. In the back of her vehicle she was carrying what looked like a large wicker picnic hamper. Inside the hamper, something was moving, noticed Leni. Something, or some *things*.

"Hi, Professor Scissorson," said Leni brightly. "Have you been looking for pigeons too?"

"I have indeed, and I think I've got something pretty special," said Professor Scissorson, climbing out and glancing at Professor Flowers's collection of birds. "I've managed to get some pink pigeons. On loan."

The Australian professor opened the little trapdoor at the top to allow Leni a peek at the birds. She had seen pink pigeons occasionally in the wild but, up close, she could see that they were exquisite. They looked like elegant doves, with bright pink beaks, soft brown wings, pale greyish-pink breasts and rust-coloured tail feathers.

Leni counted eight.

"They're beauties, aren't they?" whispered Professor Scissorson.

"Yes, and they're really rare," said Leni. "Where did you get them?"

"From a sanctuary on the north of the island," she replied. "But I've only got them for a limited time."

"Do you have both males and females?" asked Leni.

"Yes, four of each," she said confidently. "I've DNA-tested their feathers. It's the only way to know for certain." And with that she snapped shut the trapdoor and turned to Professor Flowers, who was wiping some pigeon poop off his sleeve with his hanky.

"Good luck with your...flock, Professor Flowers," she said a little rigidly. She grabbed her basket firmly by the handles and dragged it off the back of her jeep. "Light as a feather," she grimaced. In fact, it looked bulky and burdensome. But she was too proud to ask for help.

"My word!" muttered Professor Flowers. "This stuff is hard to get off."

"Come on," said Leni, feeling a bit sorry for the old man. "I'll help you get the new pigeon loft in place."

She helped him carry the DIY construction into his hut and after some pushing and shoving, it was in place. But it wasn't going to stand up on its own.

"It's okay," said the professor, undeterred. He held the wobbling structure and looked around. "Could you grab me some of those, please?" he added, indicating a pile of magazines.

Leni did as he asked and passed him several issues of a publication called *The Quill*.

The professor wedged them under the pigeon loft to prop it up.

"Splendid," he said, pleased with their efforts. "A five-star pigeon hotel."

Suddenly there was a knock at the door. "Delivery for Professor Sours!" called out a woman's voice.

"Flowers, actually," called out the professor, without looking round.

"Yes," came the woman's voice. "Flowers for Professor Sours. Where would you like them?"

The professor turned round. "Good gracious, what's this?" he exclaimed. The delivery woman was holding a huge bouquet.

"Er, thank you," he muttered, taking the massive bunch from her. "I've no idea who sent them," he said to Leni, baffled.

"Is there a note?" Leni asked.

Professor Flowers put down the bouquet and opened the small envelope that came with it.

"It just says, 'Keep up the good work'!" he said. "But it's unsigned. That's strange…"

Leni and the professor stared at the flowers and then at each other. And then, at the same time, they both thought the same thought.

"Noooooo," gasped the professor, recoiling at the idea. "They couldn't be from *her*…could they?" His eyes were as wide as an owl's.

"What on earth? Has the woman gone stark staring bonkers?" he spluttered.

And then his eyes narrowed. "One thing's for certain, Leni," he said. "I'm no pushover. If she is trying to apologize for her snooty behaviour and make friends, it won't work. Oh no!"

Had Professor Scissorson had second thoughts about their rivalry and realized they would be better off working together? If the flowers were from her, it was quite a sweet peace offering, Leni reckoned. It would mean she'd put her pride aside, and that took guts.

But what Leni and Professor Flowers didn't know was that the flowers were nothing to do with Professor Scissorson at all. They'd actually been sent by Shoober's men, Pawpaw and Beanbag. And what's more, at that very moment, the pair were just a few metres away, watching their every move.

Crouched in a makeshift jungle hideout nearby, the beady-eyed duo were wearing camouflage combat trousers and helmets. With their binoculars, they could have passed for a couple of birdwatchers. Only these birdwatchers were looking for a bird that hadn't been spotted for over three hundred years.

"The flowers have just arrived," whispered Pawpaw, looking through his binoculars.

"Let me see," said Beanbag. He brought his own binoculars up to eye level and stared ahead.

"Can't see anything," he said.

Pawpaw sighed in exasperation.

"Nope, not a thing," Beanbag went on. "It's gone totally black. Has there been an eclipse?"

"Take the lens caps off!" Pawpaw finally snapped.

"Oh, silly me!" said Beanbag. He removed the covers. "That's better." The men could see much of what the professors did through the slats of their shutters, which they hardly ever closed fully. Now Beanbag saw the bouquet that had just arrived at hut 187.

"Gorgeous flowers," cooed Beanbag. "Aaaah, pink roses, stunning birds of paradise and lovely lilies. How sweet. My mother adores lilies. Why did you send them? Is it his birthday?" Beanbag lowered his binoculars and looked at Pawpaw.

"No, you dimwit!" said his comrade. "Don't you remember? I told you before. I've bugged the flowers with a listening device. Now, let's see if it's working."

Pawpaw picked up a pair of headphones and put them on. Slowly a smile spread across his face.

"Ye-e-e-s," he said, pleased with himself. "I can hear everything."

"Go on, put yours on," he instructed Beanbag.

His partner did as he was told. Sure enough, the tiny listening bug hidden inside the blooms was working and they could hear conversation inside the hut as clear as a bell.

"I don't know who she thinks she is," they heard Professor Flowers tut.

Through the shutter slats they could make out that he was putting the stems in a vacuum flask, in pride of place on his lab bench.

Curiosity was getting the better of Leni. "I'm going next door to see her," she said, nodding towards Professor Scissorson's hut.

Professor Flowers looked uncomfortable all of a sudden. "Don't mention the flowers to her," he said. "Okay?"

"Okay!" echoed Popcorn.

The neighbouring hut's door was slightly ajar, and as soon as she popped her head round it, Leni was stunned to see that Professor Scissorson had received an identical bunch of flowers.

"Pah, he's not going to win me over with these," Leni overheard her saying while she arranged them carefully in a large vase.

"Wow, Professor, they're amazing. Who are they from?" asked Leni.

Professor Scissorson jumped. "Oh Leni, it's you! You startled me," she said. "The flowers? I've no idea who sent them. The note just says 'Keep up the good work'."

"Keep up the good work!" shrieked Popcorn.

The professor looked stonily at Leni. "So, what, is this his idea of a joke? Or does he think he can just send me flowers and I'll forget how rude he's been?"

This was strange. Same flowers. Same anonymous note. They obviously hadn't sent each other these bouquets. *But if not, who* had *sent them?* Leni wondered.

"They are beautiful," Professor Scissorson admitted, smelling the roses. "Don't even think of telling him I said that," she added quickly.

Meanwhile, not far away, Beanbag shifted in his seat. It was cramped in the little hideout. "Are we going to spend the night here?" he asked.

"Yeah, I guess so," replied Pawpaw. "We'll do it in shifts. One sleeps while the other keeps watch. Right?"

"Okay. I wish I'd known, that's all," said Beanbag.

"Why?" asked Pawpaw.

Beanbag yawned. "I'd have brought my pyjamas and teddy bear."

CHAPTER FIFTEEN
Marion and Mimi

A din of whirring and squawking woke Pawpaw at dawn the next day.

He stretched his arms in the jungle hideout, almost poking Beanbag in the eye.

"Oi, careful!" said his partner crossly.

"Morning, Beanbag. Anything to report?" asked Pawpaw. His eyelids were still half glued together.

"Not much," replied Beanbag, yawning. He'd spent the past half-hour staring at a spider, swaying in its web. He hadn't been paying attention to the professors' huts at all.

"What do you mean, not much?" said Pawpaw, wiping the sleep from his eyes and peering through the undergrowth. "They're making a racket. And look, there's smoke coming out of his place!"

Pawpaw put on his headphones, grabbed his binoculars and pointed them towards Professor Flowers's hut.

Peering through the slats, Pawpaw could see the smoke was billowing from a large stainless steel box. "Infernal flamingos!" he heard the professor shout. He was tapping the machine with his fist in frustration. "What's wrong with this thing?"

The smoke obscured his view, so Pawpaw switched a fader on a little black box from left to right to tune into the bugging device hidden in Professor Scissorson's flowers. Then he moved his binoculars across to hut 603.

Through the shutter slats, he could just about make out a white-suited figure, wearing a helmet and holding a drill in a blue-gloved hand. It was Professor Scissorson. She was hard at work drilling into a bone.

"Any sign of a dodo?" asked Beanbag nervously.

"Nah. Not yet," sighed Pawpaw.

"Oh. Well we haven't missed anything, then," said Beanbag, relieved.

The two men sat there as the tropical birds sang, the clouds flitted by and the waves rolled in and out like a never-ending hokey-cokey.

"That's better," said Professsor Flowers to Leni later that morning. He'd made some tweaks and managed to fix the gene machine. "It's what I use to roast the DNA, and release it from the proteins which bind it," he said in triumph. To Leni, it looked suspiciously like it might have once been a super-sized deep fat fryer, but she didn't say anything.

"Hang on, who's this?" Beanbag said suddenly, noticing a white golf buggy pull up outside the huts.

"Oh, just the cleaning ladies," said Pawpaw. He returned to clipping his toenails.

Outside hut 187, two ladies had stopped in their housekeeping buggy. They wore starched white uniforms and box-fresh trainers.

"Hello, Mimi and Marion!" cried out Leni.

"Hello there, Leni," trilled the ladies together. "Lovely morning!"

The two women visited every day and helped to keep

the huts spick and span. Marion was the bigger of the two, and had previously worked as a nightclub bouncer and a security guard. She had piercing brown eyes, straight white teeth and wore her hair in a huge bun on top of her head. Mimi was shorter, with a gummy grin and a high-

pitched voice. They took no nonsense, but had hearts of gold and often sang in loud, warbling voices as they worked. Both the professors were impressed by their amazing ability to clean up bird poop with their own special home-made formula, which they carried around with them in a spray bottle.

In hut 187, Professor Flowers showed them the splat on his shirt from the day before.

"One of the side effects of my job, unfortunately," he grumbled. "Bird poop gets everywhere."

"We'll have that out in no time," said Marion, examining the unsightly splodge. "No problem at all. Mimi?"

The professor looked at Mimi. "Fire away," he said, holding out the shirt.

"Bye bye, bird poop!" called Mimi, and she sprayed a couple of shots of the solution onto it. There was a smell of citrus fruit in the air and, as if by magic, the stain vanished.

"There you go, completely gone!" cheered Mimi.

The professor was impressed. "It's amazing. You've come up with a miracle formula there," he said. "Thank goodness for whatever-you-call-it. Does it have a name?"

"We haven't thought of one yet," admitted Marion.

"I've never seen anything quite like it. If I wasn't a

scientist, I'd say it was magic. What's in it?"

"That's top secret," said Mimi. "All natural ingredients, of course. But as for the details — sorry, I can't tell you."

That evening, Leni ate dinner with her parents as usual, but the atmosphere was unusually quiet. Tense, even.

"Leni, aren't those professors getting a bit carried away?" said her mum finally.

"Carried away? What do you mean?" asked Leni.

"Those pigeons squawk all day, all I hear is whirring, shouting and the sound of things being sawn up," said her mum, waving her knife around. "And I can't imagine what the inside of their huts look like. I'm worried they'll put off the other guests."

"What other guests?" remarked her dad under his breath. It was true, business wasn't exactly booming.

The fact was, they'd been happy to have any guests staying at all in the quiet low season.

"I'm learning all about DNA and genes," said Leni eagerly. "It's made me surer than ever that I want to be a vet when I grow up."

113

Her mum put her cutlery down and said, "That's wonderful, but…"

"I know they're a bit noisy, but the only people they're annoying are each other," added Leni. Her mum couldn't think of an answer to that.

It was only when Leni had walked off with the stack of dinner plates that she brought it up again with her husband. "But Roshan, she is spending *so much* time with the professors," she said. "She's ten years old. She should be playing with her friends during the holidays. I'm worried she'll blow herself up."

"She's pretty sensible," replied her dad. "And more importantly, she's happy. She's the happiest she's been in ages. This is a chance for her to be part of something special and the professors seem to like having her around. She's so excited. Just look at her face."

It was true. Leni's brown eyes sparkled and she was totally absorbed when she was helping the professors. Even when she was doing the dishes, she was miles away, thinking about dodos. Did they coo like pigeons, only in deeper voices? What did they like to eat? Were they really as chubby as the artists used to paint them in the olden days?

Her mum looked thoughtful. "I'm glad you're happy," she said when Leni came back to the table. She looked over to the fridge where a postcard with a cockatoo on the front was stuck on with magnets.

"If only Muppa was here to see you now," she added, almost to herself.

"We just heard from her by the way," said Leni's dad. He took the postcard off the fridge and read from it. "Family all well. Grandson gorgeous. Have been sharing barbecues with the kookaburras and yesterday I went for a swim with an emu. Miss you all. Love, Muppa."

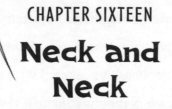

CHAPTER SIXTEEN

Neck and Neck

And so it went on. The days turned into nights, and the nights turned into days again. Leni and Popcorn popped in and out of the huts helping the two professors — feeding the pigeons, washing flasks and labelling test tubes. Both of them took her under their wing, but she was careful to be fair and help them both equally.

One afternoon, Leni was tidying up when Professor Scissorson let out a "Yay!" so loud it made her jump.

"I've done it!" cried the professor.

"Done it?" asked Leni.

"I've reconstructed the dodo genome!"

Leni was tickled pink. As pink as the professor's

pigeons. Professor Scissorson had stayed up late working on it for five nights in a row, and now her utter exhaustion was shot through with a glimmer of excitement.

Later that same day, Professor Flowers announced, "Glorious goldfinches, I've done it!" He could barely keep his eyes open, but he was almost floating on air at making the same breakthrough. "I've put the genome back together!"

This meant the race was really on, Leni thought. They were neck and neck.

"The professors would rather be anywhere than on an island with each other," she remarked to Popcorn that evening, sitting in her tree house. "The only thing keeping them here is their determination to bring back the dodo."

Popcorn bobbed his head up and down and began to preen his feathers.

"But, they have a lot in common," Leni said, looking over at their huts. She took out some seed for Popcorn and fed him.

"I wish they'd just make friends," she said. "They both want the same thing."

A few days later, she was up in her tree house again, writing a letter to Muppa, when Professor Flowers's voice interrupted her.

"Leni! Leni!" he called. "Are you out here?" Leni looked down. The professor was standing outside his hut, wearing one blue lab glove. He was squinting at the dodo tree to see if she was there.

Leni clambered down to the ground.

Professor Flowers looked pleased to see her. "Good morning, my fledgling," he said, and together with Popcorn, they went into hut 187. Inside, his pigeons were flapping, feeding and fouling anywhere they fancied. To add to the chaos, a fan was whirring at top speed, making his notes and papers flutter around like jittery doves.

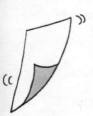

"What's the matter?" asked Leni.

"I'm in a bit of a muddle," the professor confessed. He scratched the back of his neck with his gloveless hand. Leni looked over at the bin, where he had thrown the peeled-off glove. It had missed.

"I was listening to the cricket on the radio and I injected one of the pigeon eggs with the dodo DNA," he said. "Then Winston got a hat-trick and in the excitement, I became confused. Now I can't remember which of the pigeon eggs it was."

Leni looked over at the lab bench, where there was a basket of half a dozen eggs. They all looked exactly the same.

"And to top it off, I can't find my logbook either. Oh, blithering buzzards. It's just not my day, is it?"

Leni looked around for his missing

logbook, but it was nowhere in sight. She began to search under his piles of paperwork, which were weighed down with various objects, including some of the dodo snow globes he'd bought at the market.

"Don't worry," she said. This seemed to be enough reassurance for Professor Flowers, as he slumped into a chair and put his feet up on his battered travel trunk.

"So, tell me," he said, trying to sound like he didn't care in the slightest. "Is *she* anywhere near getting an egg yet?"

"I'm not sure," said Leni casually. She picked a leaf out of her hair.

"Not sure!" squawked Popcorn, perching on the back of his chair.

Professor Flowers stroked the parakeet's green feathers. "That woman really is a thorn in my side," he sighed. "I don't know why she's so bitter. With us academics, healthy rivalry is natural. And when it's not your turn in the limelight, you just have to take it on the chin. No sulking."

He peeled off his second glove and threw it at the bin.

This time it made it in.

"Bullseye!" he shouted, clapping his hands.

"You should be proud, Leni," said Professor Flowers, "that you found those bones. Neither me nor *her*," (he nodded in the direction of Professor Scissorson's hut) "would even be doing this if you hadn't helped. Now, I just need to find that logbook."

Suddenly there was a knock at the door. Leni peered out of the shutters and mouthed "Professor Scissorson."

Professor Flowers opened the door and barricaded himself between it and outside, while Professor Scissorson craned her neck in an attempt to see in. "I don't mean to be a sticky-beak," she lied. "I just wondered if Leni's here?"

"Leni's here!" squawked Popcorn.

"I'll take that as a yes," said Professor Scissorson. "Leni!" she called. "Could you come over and help me with something? Whenever you get a moment? Like now?"

"Just coming," said Leni, appearing at the door. "See you soon, Professor Flowers!"

No sooner were they inside hut 603 than Professor Scissorson was asking her, "So, what's the prof up to?"

"Oh just the usual," said Leni vaguely. She felt uncomfortable talking about each to the other so she stayed tight-lipped whenever they tried to get information from her. She twirled her hair around her index finger.

"Hmm, never mind," said Professor Scissorson. "Look, Leni, I have something really exciting to show you."

She led Leni round the back of the hut to the pigeon loft. Hers was not as ramshackle as Professor Flowers's. She had installed a walk-in aviary made of black wire mesh panels, with a door. Each bird had a cubbyhole to roost in, and they shared an area out front, a sort of pigeon-playground.

In one of the compartments sat an elegant pink pigeon. His cubbyhole was labelled "Lionel". Professor Scissorson gently lifted the side of his pinkish-grey belly. There, lying on a bed of straw underneath the bird was a beautiful white egg.

"Wow," gasped Leni. "Have you, have you...?"

"Yes," breathed the professor. "I've injected this little

egg with my reconstructed dodo DNA. Now we wait. And hope."

Leni looked at the egg and felt amazed. It was quite small, smaller than a hen's egg, but what was inside could be making history.

"Lionel is stepping up to the role of dad and he is doing a fantastic job of keeping the egg warm," said the professor. "He sits on it all day and then at dusk, Loretta, the mum-to-be, takes over and sits on the egg all night." Professor Scissorson let go of Lionel's belly and gave him a gentle stroke on the head.

Leni clenched her fists and started jumping around. "Ooh I can't wait! I just can't!" she cried.

"Just can't!" parroted Popcorn.

Then she thought of Professor Flowers next door in 187. The kindly old man getting in a flap looking for his precious logbook. She wondered how he'd feel about the fact that Professor Scissorson already had a pigeon sitting on her dodo DNA-injected egg.

A glum feeling took the edge off her glee and Leni stopped bounding around. "What's the matter?" asked Professor Scissorson.

"Oh nothing, it's just Professor Flowers…he…"

"So he's not reached this stage, then?" guessed Professor Scissorson, her hands on her hips. "Well, he'll be disappointed. He's bound to be. But you can't win them all, can you?"

"I suppose not," said Leni.

"Anyway, let's not count our chickens," cautioned the professor. "Or our dodos for that matter. I can inject more eggs if this one doesn't go the distance. But this is the first. Let's wait to see if it hatches into a live baby bird — a squab. I so hope it does."

"Me too," said Leni.

"Me too!" chirped Popcorn.

Leni leaned in and gently lifted Lionel's belly to get another look at the egg he was guarding so closely. "Come on, little dodo chick," she whispered. "Keep growing strong."

CHAPTER SEVENTEEN

Talking Turkey

Outside, in the bushes, Pawpaw grabbed Beanbag's sleeve. "Let's get up to HQ right away," he said. A fiendish smile crept across his lips. "The dodo has landed."

"But dodos can't fly…" began Beanbag.

Pawpaw swiped him with a rolled-up comic. "You doughnut! Come on, let's go."

Up at Shoober's mansion, the Sugar King was in his drawing room, posing for his latest portrait. He was sitting on a gold-plated "throne", wearing a crown on his head and swathed in a purple robe. In one hand he held a piece of raw sugar cane, and in the other, a golden sugar bowl — like a newly crowned monarch holding a sceptre and orb.

"Hold still, sir. That's it," said the artist painting him. He was putting the finishing touches to Shoober's head on the canvas. "Just a little longer."

Meanwhile, his wife Giavanna was lounging on the couch, talking into her mobile phone.

"That sounds amazing, sweetie," she cooed. "I can't wait. Catch up soon, honey. Bye bye."

"What was that?" asked Shoober through his forced smile.

"Oh nothing important. Just a new face mask I'm going to try. Apparently, it completely rejuvenates the skin and banishes fine lines." She smoothed the corners of her mouth with the pads of her fingers.

"What's in it?"

"Snail slime."

Shoober almost dropped his sugar bowl. "Hold still," the artist ordered.

"You could use some too," Giavanna rasped, noticing that her husband's forehead had crumpled up. Her gold earrings jangled as she rose from the couch. "I'm off to get my nails done now, then it's the hairdresser, then lunch and a massage. It's non-stop, honey! I'll see you tonight." She tottered off in her high heels, leaving the pungent, musky smell of her perfume in her wake.

"Perfect," declared the artist to his subject. "You can relax now."

Shoober was just taking off his crown when Pawpaw came running in so quickly he had to skid to a halt, almost knocking over the artist and his easel.

"Boss, we got news for you," he gasped.

"Oh yeah?" asked Shoober, raising an eyebrow. He signalled for the artist to pack up and leave.

"We gotta talk turkey," said Beanbag.

"Dodo actually," said Pawpaw.

Shoober got up from his throne, moved to the couch, sat down again and lit a cigar. "What's happened?" he asked. "Have those crazy scientists made a dodo yet?"

"Not quite, but one of them, the woman, has just injected an egg with dodo DNA," said Pawpaw. "And now it's growing into a dodo chick. There's a pigeon sitting on it."

This got Shoober's back up. Really. The hair on his back actually began to stand up on end. Maybe it was static electricity from the robe. Anyway, he started thinking about dodos waddling all over the land *he* wanted. He glanced down at that day's edition of the

Mauritian Pigeon Post, which was lying on the coffee table. The headline read:

ANCIENT JUNGLE SET ASIDE FOR PRECIOUS PINK PIGEONS

"Dratted eco-warriors, I hate the lot of them!" he fumed. "First the kestrel, then the parakeet. Now the pink pigeon! Mark my words. If those goofy dodos come back again, they'll be sure to designate a 'dodo protection zone' or whatever, for them too."

He turned to the men. Pawpaw was picking his nose and rolling the contents between his finger and thumb. Beanbag was looking out of the window at a gardener who was busy constructing the word "Giavanna" out of white flowers in a nearby bed.

"Well then?" said Shoober, his eyebrows raised.

"What are you waiting for?" he shouted, getting up suddenly from the couch. "I want that egg! Get it and bring it to me!"

"But how?" asked Beanbag.

Pawpaw elbowed him.

"Think of something! That's what I pay you for, Beanbag!" thundered Shoober, waving his cigar. "You're supposed to be the best henchmen in the business."

"Are we?" said Beanbag, flattered. "That's sweet. Who said that?"

"Enough! I want that egg," Shoober declared. "You work out the details."

As he spoke, a strange, acrid smell reached his nostrils. He shrivelled up his nose. Where could it be coming from? He looked down. A small hole had started forming where an ember from his cigar had landed on the purple robe. And it was getting larger.

"Argh!" cried Shoober. "My robe! It's on fire!" In a flash, Pawpaw grabbed a vase of roses, pulled out the stems and threw the water all over Shoober.

"It's okay, boss, it's out," gasped Pawpaw.

He looked pleased with himself. But Shoober was drenched in foul-smelling water and his sodden cigar hung limply from his mouth. He was seething.

"Get. Out. Of. Here. Now…" he said quietly.

But they were so scared they couldn't move. Shoober took the volume up several notches.

"Did you hear me? SCRAM!"

The pair made their exit and Shoober dripped stinking, stale flower-water across the hallway to the bathroom. He took off his soggy robe and swapped it for a fluffy leopard-print towel. He caught sight of a framed photo on the wall. It was of him shaking hands with the Mauritian president.

"I didn't get where I am today by giving in to no dumb birds," he muttered, his damp cigar still clamped between his teeth. "And I sure as sugar ain't gonna start now."

CHAPTER EIGHTEEN

Shirley
and Pauline

The following week, Leni was up in her tree house, making up a poem about birds in her notebook. She heard the golf buggy approaching and glanced down as the cleaners arrived for their daily visit. Then she did a double take.

The cleaners got out of the buggy and hauled their cleaning crates into hut 603, but something looked different about them, Leni thought. Then she realized why. It wasn't Marion and Mimi.

"Sorry, they're both a bit tied up right now," explained one of the new cleaners to Professor Scissorson. She had a large forehead, slicked-back black hair and a dimple in the middle of her chin.

"Tied up?" repeated Professor Scissorson.

"Yes. They're, er, taking part in a sponsored clean-a-thon."

"A clean-a-thon?"

"Yes," replied the dimple-chinned woman. "They're cleaning non-stop...to raise money for charity."

"Good on them," Professor Scissorson said. "Which charity?"

"The, er, Save the Clothes Peg Foundation."

"What?"

"Yes, they're critically endangered. In danger of being replaced by tumble dryers. We want to conserve the clothes peg and its unique way of life," said the slick-haired lady.

Professor Scissorson nodded politely but didn't have a clue what the woman was talking about.

"Don't worry, Prof," said the other lady, who was shorter than her colleague and had rosy cheeks. "Your hut will still be cleaned. We're the supply cleaners. I'm Shirley, but you can call me Shirl."

Shirley grasped the professor's hand and shook it.

"And I'm Paw …Paw…Pauline. Pleased to meet you too," announced the larger lady, extending her hand. The professor had never seen such hairy arms. "What, er, sweet tattoos," she blurted out, noticing the cleaner's knuckles. "Thanks," said Pauline. "I, ahem, I chose them because I *love* cleaning and *hate*…dirt."

"How lovely," smiled Professor Scissorson as her hand was crushed in the woman's powerful grip.

"Well, no time to lose… let's get to work!" the woman trilled, or at least tried to.

Her words came out cracked and strained.

"Oh dear. Have you got a sore throat?"

"Er, yes," coughed Pauline gruffly. "Man flu."

"Man flu?" repeated the professor, not sure she'd heard her right.

"Um, uh, I mean it's a cold," replied Pauline. "It just makes my voice seem all, er, manly..."

There was something odd about these two, and Professor Scissorson couldn't quite work out what it was, but she noticed that Shirley didn't seem to know how to put together a vacuum cleaner. She grappled with it bare-fisted, as if she were fighting a dancing octopus. Then she gave up and attempted to iron the bed sheets, which were still on the bed.

Meanwhile, in the bathroom, Pauline was using the toilet brush to clean the bath and the professor's toothbrush to clean the toilet. She emerged a few minutes later, took a feather duster and proceeded to dust all the items in the fridge with it, including the salad.

"Please be careful not to touch my lab equipment, okay?" said the professor.

"Right you are, Prof," grinned Shirley. She was attempting to clean the sofa using a mop.

Professor Scissorson was right to be suspicious. For the "supply cleaners" who had arrived at hut 603 that morning were not really cleaners at all. They were, in fact, Pawpaw and Beanbag, disguised in cleaners' uniforms and wearing make-up.

The henchmen had hijacked Marion and Mimi's housekeeping buggy at the top of the road. Right now, the poor cleaners were sitting under a tree not too far away, with their hands tied and their mouths gagged.

The professor thought the new cleaners had some unusual working methods, but she had important work to get on with herself, so she left them to it and sat down at her computer.

As soon as she was out of earshot, Pawpaw grabbed Beanbag's arm. "There's no time to lose!" he urged. "Now what was the name of that pigeon again? Lorna? Linda? Leonard?"

Beanbag tucked his cleaning cloth into his apron pocket.

"Lionel," he said.

They checked out the loft where the pink pigeons were nesting.

"But the professor's still here," Beanbag said out of the corner of his mouth. "How can we distract her?"

"Don't worry, I'll think of something," whispered Pawpaw.

"Oh my word, this cold!" he shrilled in his Pauline voice. "My nose is streaming. I'm so sorry, Professor, but do you have any tissues?" He sniffed loudly.

"Of course," said Professor Scissorson, getting up. "They're in the bathroom."

While she was out of the room, Pawpaw and Beanbag tiptoed over to the pigeon loft.

"Which of you is Lionel?" whispered Pawpaw desperately. He scanned the names on the compartments: Judy, Martha, Ingrid, Loretta, Kevin, Ozzy, Lionel.

"Lionel! This is the one," he said. "I'll lift up his belly, you grab the egg. Okay?"

Pawpaw gently prised up the pigeon's underbelly, and sure enough, the little egg was tucked in there.

Cautiously, Beanbag went to take it. But Lionel pecked him sharply on the wrist.

"Ooooww," howled Beanbag. "Dratted pigeon!"

"What's that?" called Professor Scissorson from the bathroom.

"Oh, nothing!" called Pawpaw in his falsetto voice. "It's just that my runny nose has...splatted...a smidgeon...on the floor. I'll clean it up straight away."

Pawpaw held Lionel's beak while Beanbag gently picked up the egg. He wrapped it carefully in his dusting cloth and placed it in his apron pocket, managing not to break it in the process.

No sooner had he popped it in its hiding place than Professor Scissorson was back. "Here you are, Pauline," she said, passing Pawpaw a box of tissues.

"Thanks," he said and immediately took one out, stuck his nose into it and blew so hard it almost made his earrings fall off. "Well, we're done here," he smiled. "We'd better be going."

"Already?" said the professor, surprised.

"My doctor told me not to overdo it, you know," said Pawpaw hurriedly, waving the used tissue uselessly. "I shouldn't really be working at all with this cold, but we didn't want to let you down."

The two bogus cleaners made their way out, dragging the vacuum cleaner and mop behind them. They couldn't get to their buggy fast enough. After dumping their gear in the back, they leaped straight into the front. They were just about to take off when they were cut short.

"Ladies!" called Professor Scissorson from the front deck. "Hold on just a moment!"

The impostors looked at each other through their fake eyelashes in dread. Had they been rumbled?

"Uh, yes, Prof?" said Beanbag in his sweetest Shirley voice.

There was a pause. "You left this behind," said Professor Scissorson. She walked up to the buggy and handed Beanbag the feather duster.

"Oh, silly us!" giggled Beanbag. He took the duster from the professor and threw it over his shoulder into the back.

"And I hope your cold clears up soon, Pauline," Professor Scissorson said to Pawpaw politely.

"Thank you," he sniffed. "Goodbye!"

Pawpaw pressed his foot on the accelerator pedal and they were off. Not exactly at breakneck pace, but they were off nonetheless. And with the precious dodo egg safely cradled in Beanbag's apron, the dirty duo made a clean getaway.

CHAPTER NINETEEN

A Poached Egg

As the cleaners were leaving, Leni looked down from her tree house. She noticed something strange about the way they walked back to their buggy. The shorter one waddled like a baby duck while the taller one hulked along like an emperor penguin.

She climbed down and made her way to Professor Scissorson's hut. Popcorn followed and perched on the deck.

"Hi, Leni," the professor said, watching the cleaners drive away. "Hmm, there was definitely something odd about those ladies," she remarked. "Did your mum and dad say there would be supply cleaners here today?"

"I don't remember them mentioning it," said Leni.

"Well it wasn't Marion and Mimi," replied Professor Scissorson. "It's a shame. Those two weren't nearly as thorough. And they left without doing *his* hut," she added, nodding towards number 187.

"Talking of Professor Flowers, where *is* he?" asked Leni.

"No idea. I've not seen him at all this morning," Professor Scissorson replied.

"Maybe he's gone for a swim in the lagoon," suggested Leni.

"Maybe," said Professor Scissorson. They both looked out but there was no sign of the English professor in the dazzling, peacock-blue water.

Leni sighed. "How is the egg today?" she asked. "And the pigeons?"

Professor Scissorson smiled. "Let's go and have a look, shall we?" she said.

They went into the hut and the professor headed straight to Lionel's cubbyhole. She gently lifted the pigeon's underbelly to check.

"My egg!" she shrieked. "It's gone!"

"What?" said Leni, thinking the professor must be mistaken. She craned her neck to examine the roosting spot.

Professor Scissorson rummaged around underneath Lionel's feathered belly, but still, no egg.

Panicking, she desperately checked under all the other pigeons' bellies, and the sleeping ones cooed abruptly at the disturbance.

"It can't have just vanished. That's impossible," she cried. Sweat was starting to appear on her forehead.

"Impossible! Impossible!" screeched Popcorn.

"Shhhhh," Leni urged him.

"My dodo egg!" the professor screamed, grasping her hair. "My dodo egg! Where is it?"

But Lionel just sat there, as if nothing was wrong.

"Let's think about this logically," said Leni.

"Could anybody have stolen it?"

There was silence for a moment, and then the professor's eyes went owly as a terrible thought occurred to her.

"Flowers," she seethed under her breath.

Leni shook her head. "No, no, I don't think..."

"It can only have been Flowers," she fumed. "I knew it! That man has been plotting this the whole time. As soon as he knew I had an egg, he stole it from under my nose."

"Hold on a minute..." began Leni.

"And now he's disappeared!" continued Professor Scissorson. "He's taken off with my egg."

"Just a..."

"He can't fool me. I'm on to him. It's a low-down trick, but I'm..."

"Life is sweet!" shrilled Popcorn.

Professor Scissorson swung round to where he was perched on the back of a chair. "What?"

"Life is sweet! Life is sweet!" repeated the bird, getting more and more worked up.

"Life is sweet," said Leni quietly to herself. They'd heard it on the radio, on the TV and it was plastered across every ad for Shoober Sugar. But why was Popcorn saying it now?

And then, in a flash, Leni knew what he was trying so hard to tell them.

"Professor Scissorson," she said, doing her best to stay calm. "You said there was something odd about the cleaners today?"

"Well, as a matter of fact, there was. They left greasy fingermarks on the mirror and..."

"Maybe those supply cleaners weren't supply cleaners at all," said Leni.

"What?" gulped Professor Scissorson.

"I think I know who's behind this," Leni continued.

"Who?" asked the professor.

"Benny Shoober," she answered gravely.

"Shoober!" squawked Popcorn. He nodded his green head so fiercely Leni thought he might fall off the back of the chair.

"Eh? Benny Shoo-who?" said Professor Scissorson, perplexed.

"Shoober. S-H-O-O-B-E-R," said Leni. "He's a big sugar tycoon, owns lots of land on the island. And he hates birds. Especially rare ones. He thinks they get in the way of his greedy schemes. I wouldn't be surprised if he's heard about your dodo and sent his men here to steal the egg."

The professor was so agog, all she could manage was a faint-sounding, "Men?"

"That's right. Those two cleaners were no ladies. And if the Sugar King is up to no good," added Leni, "we're going to make sure he doesn't get away with it."

Professor Scissorson had her head in her hands.

"Don't worry, Professor," said Leni. "We're going to get your egg back."

CHAPTER TWENTY

Chez Shoober

Questions started to swim around Leni's mind like the fish darting through the coral reef in the lagoon nearby.

But they had to get moving. "Professor Scissorson, I think I know where the egg is," said Leni. "Got your car keys?"

In an instant, Professor Scissorson grabbed her hat and keys, and they dashed to her jeep parked outside. Leni was still closing her passenger door as the professor sped off. She skidded, swerved and bounced over some very large potholes. Popcorn flew close behind them.

"Benny Shoober is the most powerful sugar magnate in Mauritius and there are always rumours flying around about him," Leni explained on the journey. "He has a bad reputation — he doesn't pay his workers very well, and he is obsessed with buying up more and more land. He lives on a huge estate, in a mansion with gold-plated telephones, toilets and even toenail clippers. His wife, Giavanna, is the most pampered woman you could ever meet. She flies to Paris to buy perfume and has a shoe cupboard the size of an aircraft hangar."

"Well, if he's taken my egg, he is in for a surprise," said Professor Scissorson with determination. "Benny Shoober picked the wrong woman to mess with."

"And I don't know what his henchmen have done with Marion and Mimi," said Leni. "I just hope they're safe."

"And Professor Flowers too," added Professor Scissorson, biting her lip.

Soon they came to the front gates of the Shoober estate. "What shall we do with the jeep?" asked Leni.

"I'll hide it in the bushes," decided the professor, and she drove it headlong into some nearby undergrowth. After switching off the engine, the pair clambered out of the vehicle and through the tangled plants.

"Let's find a way in before someone sees us," said the professor.

There didn't seem to be anyone about, and Leni was surprised that the front gates weren't even locked.

They crept along the sweeping front drive. "Is that him?" asked Professsor Scissorson, pointing to the large statue just in front of the entrance.

"That's him," said Leni.

"Bald as a coot, isn't he?"

The house was enormous and above the front door, they noticed the words "Chez Shoober" engraved in gold lettering.

But Leni and Professor Scissorson made their way round to the back of the property by creeping among the shady trees and bushes which edged the gardens. That way, reckoned the professor, they'd be less likely to be spotted from inside.

"Look at that," said Leni, pointing at an ornamental fountain featuring a baby cupid standing by the side of a shallow pool.

"My word," said Professor Scissorson. "He looks like

he's doing…a…you know…"

"A wee," giggled Leni. "He looks like he's doing a wee."

"Doing a wee!" sang out Popcorn.

"Ssssh," Leni giggled to the bird. Just then, she spotted a partially-open window on the ground floor, so she encouraged Popcorn to fly over and check the coast was clear. Then, they scurried across the lawn as fast as they could and clambered in through the window.

The room smelled of flowers and there was a bunch of newly-cut blooms in a large glass vase on a table. There were Persian rugs and potted palms, a sparkling chandelier and shiny satin sofas with leopard-print cushions and gold tassels. They had climbed into the Shoobers' drawing room.

Leni tiptoed over to the door, listened closely for a moment, and then gently turned the gold handle to peep out into the hallway. She gave a thumbs-up sign and Professor Scissorson clomped across the wooden floorboards in her big boots. "Ssssh," shushed Leni. "Someone might hear you."

They made their way into the large hallway, which boasted as its centrepiece a golden statue of Giavanna, in the image of a Roman goddess. Gold-framed photographs of the Shoobers hung on the walls. There was one of Benny playing golf, one of him scuba diving, one of him skiing, and another of him surfing. "Pffft, he's got his wetsuit on the wrong way round," snorted Professor Scissorson when she saw it.

"Wrong way round!" squawked Popcorn. Leni gently

grabbed his beak. "Sorry, Popcorn," she whispered, "but you've *got* to stay quiet. You just have to. *Please.*" She let go and he seemed to get the message.

"The egg must be here somewhere," she went on, looking around. And then she smelled cigar smoke. It was coming from the other side of the hallway. Together, she and Professor Scissorson crept towards it, the whirring of ceiling fans the only thing that deadened the sound of their footsteps.

Daring to peek through the open, oak-panelled door of the room, Leni saw that it was an office. There was a large desk with a fountain pen in a holder, a pile of books with "*Success is Sweet*" embossed on their spines, a gold-plated telephone and an ashtray. In it, the cigar was smouldering away.

And then they both saw what they'd come for.

"There it is," Leni whispered. "Under the lamp."

Sure enough, resting in a little golden bowl of paperclips was the egg.

CHAPTER TWENTY-ONE

Caught

The egg was sitting in the glare of the spotlight, like a nervous performer in a talent show.

"That rotten thief!" fumed Professor Scissorson. And before Leni could stop her, she strode over to the desk. Her hand was poised over the egg, but just as she was about to grab it, the gold phone began to ring.

"*Riiiiiing, ring, riiiiiing, ring—*"

"Riii—" Popcorn started to mimic it, but Leni shot him a look which said, "Don't you dare."

Professor Scissorson froze to the spot, not knowing what to do as the phone rang on and on for what seemed like ages.

Someone would come in soon to answer it. Knowing they had no time to lose, Leni reached over and grasped the little white egg. It felt warm from the lamp's heat.

Then, the phone stopped ringing.

"We've got to get out of here," whispered Leni.

The professor jolted out of her daze. "Right-o," she said, and they turned to make their getaway.

"Well, well, well, what do we have here?" snarled a voice. "Looks like we have some uninvited guests."

"And they're making themselves right at home," added his partner.

Barricading the office doorway were Pawpaw and Beanbag.

"What do you have there in your hand, little girl?" asked Pawpaw. He loomed over Leni like an eagle over a rabbit.

"Leave her alone!" shouted Professor Scissorson. "What did you think you were playing at, 'Pauline'? Coming to my hut and stealing my egg? How dare you!"

"What do you mean, Pauline?" asked Pawpaw.

"Don't play dumb with me," seethed the professor.

"It's written right there on your knuckles. *Love* cleaning and *hate* dirt, do you? Oh come *on*. And you, 'Shirley'!" she spat at Beanbag. "You ought to be ashamed of yourself."

"Why, was my dusting not up to scratch?" asked Beanbag. He blinked rapidly and everyone stared at his fluttering eyelids. Pawpaw kicked him in the shins. That was it. They'd been rumbled.

"You idiot!" Pawpaw snarled under his breath to his partner. "You're still wearing your fake eyelashes."

Beanbag ripped them off so fast he howled out in pain.

Leni stepped forward. "This is the professor's egg, and you had no right to steal it," she said, hoping they couldn't hear her voice shaking. "We are taking back what is ours."

"I don't think so, little girl," said Pawpaw. "Give me the egg."

Just then, a furious ball of feathers hit him square in the face. It was Popcorn, and he began to peck wildly at Pawpaw's nose, ears, anything he could reach.

155

"Wretched bird, get off! Get *off*!" blundered Pawpaw.

The professor and Leni made a run for it. The two henchmen gave chase. The pair ran as fast as they could, but no sooner had they made it to the hallway and headed for the front door, than Leni tripped on the edge of a Persian rug. The precious egg flew out of her hand and up into the air. It soared in a smooth, upward arc.

As it came down again, Leni groaned in agony. They'd got so close. Could it all be over for the poor dodo? Before it had even had a second chance?

In a flash, a chubby, gold-ringed hand appeared. And the precious egg fell right into the outstretched palm of Benny Shoober.

CHAPTER TWENTY-TWO
A Rotten Egg

Lying on the hallway floor, Leni was aware of a woolly sensation in her mouth. But in a jiffy, Beanbag pulled her up off the rug, grabbed her arms and held them behind her back in a firm grasp. Pawpaw wasted no time in grabbing Professor Scissorson's arms and doing the same to her.

"Ow, let go," winced Leni, spitting out bits of fluff.

But Benny Shoober ignored her plea. "How kind of you both to visit," said the tycoon with an evil smile on his face. He cradled the dodo egg in his palm.

"Give back our egg, NOW!" shouted the professor.

"Now, now, that's no way to speak to your host,"

said Shoober in a voice so calm it was menacing.

"I am curious, how did you know I had the egg?" he continued. He strolled around the statue of his wife and then fixed Leni with a stare. She pinched her lips together as if she might accidentally blurt it out. But her eyes darted to Popcorn, giving the game away anyway.

"Ah, the bird, was it?" said Shoober, glancing up at Popcorn. "Hmm, I don't like birds. Especially ones that squawk."

"Squawk!" repeated Popcorn, who had perched on the head of Giavanna's statue, out of Shoober's reach.

"He almost pecked my eyes out too, boss," complained Pawpaw.

"Why did you steal the egg?" demanded Leni. "You don't even like birds."

"You're right, I don't," answered Shoober simply. "And a silly, oversized pigeon is the last thing I want. It would only get in the way of my plans."

This was what Leni had dreaded. Shoober didn't want to keep the dodo, he wanted to destroy it.

"I'm afraid your dodo bird would be too...

inconvenient," he said carefully. "If it returns, those misguided eco-idiots will want to give it a piece of the jungle. I cannot allow a fat, flightless fool to scupper my plans for more fields of sweet, sweet sugar.

"And so the ridiculous bird must be destroyed before it can hatch!" he declared.

Leni was sure he was going to crush the egg right in front of them. "Noooo," she cried out. "Don't do it... *PLEASE*."

To her surprise, Shoober stopped. "No, you're right," he said. "I don't want to get egg white all over my rings. I'm going to take it to the Granulator."

That didn't sound any better than being crushed to death in his merciless fist. "What is the Granulator?" asked Leni. Her arms were beginning to ache but she wasn't going to give up without a fight.

"Why don't you come and see for yourselves?" said Shoober, sweet as a lemon. He nodded to Pawpaw and Beanbag. "Bring them up to the Granulator."

CHAPTER TWENTY-THREE

The Granulator

Benny Shoober turned on his heel and walked out of the hallway, through the grand double doors at the front of the mansion and around to the vast sugar refinery. His henchmen frogmarched Leni and Professor Scissorson along in his wake, but in their haste, Popcorn was left behind. He let out a desperate caw but it was too late, the double doors swung back and imprisoned him. He watched in vain as they disappeared from view.

The Shoober Sugar factory wasn't far from the mansion and it had two huge chimneys which billowed steam. This was the place where workers brought mountains of raw sugar cane and transformed it into mountains of sugar — and money — for the tycoon.

They soon reached the main warehouse, where Shoober pressed some buttons on a keypad.

"You and the workers, take the afternoon off," he barked to somebody on the intercom. Then he added with a purr, "My treat."

A few minutes later they were inside, and met with the sight of a working sugar factory in full swing. Cogs were rotating, drums were whirring, and steam was puffing out of the various vats around them. "Follow me," said Shoober, still clutching the egg.

He approached a set of blue steel stairs, which led to an elevated walkway running across the warehouse. They were marched up the stairs, and came to a stop where the walkway widened out into a small platform near the centre of the whole operation.

Leni imagined that a sugar factory might look like a giant sweet shop, but nothing about this place looked yummy or tasty. Vats held sludgy substances in shades of stagnant pond green, murky mustard and curdled cream. Nearby, a giant rotating cylinder was throwing clods of something that looked like dried mud onto a conveyor belt. A huge tank with a little porthole window offered a snapshot view of some bubbling brown liquid. Above their heads, colossal bulk bags of sugar were lifted by a hoist and carried across the ceiling to a platform on the far side of the warehouse. It looked like the sort of place a human being could meet a nasty end, Leni thought. What chance did a little egg stand?

"Welcome to my factory," announced Shoober. "This is where the magic happens."

He studied the egg in his hand. "But not for everybody. Today we say goodbye to our friend the dodo. I'm sorry, but you're extinct already, so really, what difference does it make?" A cruel smile formed on his lips.

"And take comfort in this: the Granulator is very quick."

He was standing alongside the top of a large blue storage tank, with a trap door set into it. "The Granulator is like a big centrifuge," Shoober explained, opening the hatch. Leni recalled the centrifuge she'd unpacked for Professor Scissorson back at her hut. This was in a totally different league. She looked down at the monstrous, spinning drum inside, where sugar was whirring at supersonic speed, and caught her breath.

"The sugar cane comes up to the machine," said Shoober, pointing to a wide conveyor belt that was steadily bringing it upwards. "When it goes into the centrifuge, the force of the spinning separates the sugar into crystals and molasses. Molasses is a by-product of the sugar-making process." He pointed to another tank nearby, the one containing the brown gloopy-looking liquid behind the porthole.

Professor Scissorson narrowed her eyes and, in a terse voice, said, "Thanks for the guided tour. But you're not putting my egg in there."

Shoober just smirked. "I like a sweet coffee," he

replied. "Who knows? Maybe I'll stir it into my espresso tomorrow morning. That's it. A dodo egg-spresso!" He chuckled at his own joke.

"The dodo hasn't even had a second chance at life and you want to destroy it!" exclaimed Professor Scissorson. "And for what? For money. Is that all you care about? Money?" She wriggled in frustration but Pawpaw just gripped her more tightly.

"Silence!" shouted Shoober. The buttons of his shirt strained under his belly as he puffed out his chest like a rooster. "I am the mighty Benny Shoober. And nobody messes with me."

The tycoon held the egg over the gaping open chasm, about to drop the dodo to its doom.

Leni's despair was tearing her apart. How could this be happening? The dodo's de-extinction had started in a mini centrifuge. Now it looked like it was about to be re-extincted in a giant one.

And then, out of the corner of her eye, Leni saw something moving across the ceiling. Could it be one of the factory workers? She looked up.

But it wasn't any of the factory workers. Instead, trundling towards them in three giant sugar bags suspended from the ceiling, were Marion, Mimi and Professor Flowers. They swooped down from above like three brave superheroes (only in slow motion). The professor was in the middle bag, flanked by Marion and Mimi — both armed with mops.

"What the?" gasped the gobsmacked Shoober. But the cleaners had already jumped out of their bags.

"Gotcha!" yelled Marion. The pair clobbered the two henchmen on the head, knocking them out in an instant. They slumped to the floor, releasing Leni and Professor Scissorson.

The cleaners then threw their mops into the gaping centrifuge and with an unhealthy groan, the huge machine ground to a halt.

The shocked Sugar King was rooted to the spot. Seizing his chance, Professor Flowers clambered out of his bulk bag and swiped the egg right out of Benny Shoober's palm. And in his politest English accent, he said, "I think you'll find this is Professor Scissorson's, old chap."

CHAPTER TWENTY-FOUR

Happy Birthday

"Professor Flowers!" whooped Leni. Professor Scissorson's jaw dropped. But Benny Shoober's entire face seemed to suffer a landslide. The cleaners grabbed the tycoon and put him in a double armlock.

"Let me go!" Shoober shouted. The Sugar King was strong, but he was no match for the brute force of the cleaning women, strengthened by years of vacuuming, scrubbing and mopping.

"How dare you take my egg?" Shoober barked at Professor Flowers.

"It's not yours, actually," replied the old man brightly. "And now I'm returning it to its rightful owner." And with that, Professor Flowers stretched out his arm to Professor Scissorson, and said, "I think this egg belongs to you."

Professor Scissorson was totally bowled over and, with a trembling hand, she took the egg.

Underneath them, Leni noticed that the tank of molasses was making gurgling noises and a small amber light on its side had started to flash. Through the little porthole, Leni could see the gloop getting angrier.

Then she looked at the egg in Professor Scissorson's hand. Was she seeing things, or were there a couple of hairline cracks just starting to appear?

"The dodo!" she exclaimed. "It's starting to hatch!"

Leni noticed a buzz of excitement between the two professors. They'd both seen a lot of eggs hatch in their time, but none quite like this one. Meanwhile, Shoober squirmed, trying to escape the cleaners. "Stay still, you," growled Marion. "You're not going anywhere."

And then, before their very eyes, out of the little white eggshell, a tiny, tiny beak emerged. Ever so slowly, a little damp-feathered wingtip poked out. Then the entire wing, a head and finally the body of a baby bird emerged and flopped onto Professor Scissorson's outstretched palm, as if it had just finished a mammoth race. Here it was — the world's first de-extincted dodo.

The professor had tears in her eyes. "My precious baby," she cried, cradling the new hatchling. The squab had wet, grey down and big dark eyes, with the lids still closed. Leni had never seen anything so beautiful.

"It's the cutest thing ever. Look at its gangly legs and tucked-in little wings," marvelled Leni. "But you can tell

it's a dodo. Check out the shape of its beak. It couldn't be anything else!"

"*Her* beak," said Professor Scissorson.

Professor Flowers looked at her.

"Are you sure?" he asked.

"Dead set," she replied. "I DNA-tested the egg before it hatched, to find out."

The dodo was alive and kicking. And she was hungry. "We've got to get the squab back to her adoptive mum and dad as soon as possible," said Professor Scissorson.

Shoober was glowering, but in the firm grip of the cleaners and with his two henchmen out cold at his feet, there was nothing he could do.

"This sucks!" he shouted, stamping his foot. "Who needs dumb dodos? Or kestrels, or parakeets or pesky pink pigeons? Have you all gone MAD? The world has enough silly birds! What we need is sugar! More sweet, sensational, scrumptious sugar!

"You'll regret the day you ever de-extincted the dodo," he snarled. "You maniacs! And you!" he addressed Marion and Mimi. "You will pay for this. I'll ruin you and your business! I'll make sure you never clean another toilet on this island!"

Leni half expected to hear Popcorn squawk "Island!" and then she realized he wasn't there. "Where's Popcorn?" she said. A bad feeling started creeping into her stomach and it churned like the molasses in the tank.

CHAPTER TWENTY-FIVE

Dodo Mumbo Jumbo

An eerie silence hung in the vast warehouse, broken only by the occasional sound of bubbling gloop. Leni tried to think back to when she'd last seen Popcorn.

"Is this what you're looking for?" Everybody spun round to see a figure in thigh-high leopard-print boots and a pink miniskirt. She had enormous earrings, huge hair, and larger-than-life lips. She stood there pouting and holding a golden bird cage. It was Giavanna.

"Popcorn!" shouted Leni. She started to run to the parakeet. "Thank goodness you're safe."

"Not so fast, little girl," said Giavanna in her scratchy-sweet voice. She gripped the cage tightly.

"I think you have something I want..."

A new dread crept into Leni's heart. Oh no, what could she be after? Shoober looked relieved. "Thank you for coming to get me, sweetlips," he sighed.

"It's not you I'm after," snapped Giavanna. To Leni's surprise, she turned her gaze on the baby dodo. "It's this little beauty I want," she purred.

Shoober was stupefied. "But sweetlips, please! You've got to help me," he cried.

"Quit jabbering, you idiot," she shot back.

Giavanna bent down and brought her face up to the baby bird in Professor Scissorson's hand. The professor instinctively tried to pull back, but the woman gripped her wrist with her long-taloned fingers. Leni thought she was going to kiss the dodo but she simply breathed on her. She seemed besotted by the hatchling.

Releasing her grip, Giavanna stood up straight again and said, "I don't know what my husband was thinking, trying to destroy this beautiful bird." She threw a withering glance at him. "What a tragedy that would have been."

Leni breathed a sigh of relief.

"She's an exquisite creature," Giavanna carried on. "I want this dodo for myself. And she is going to be kept very much alive."

Now Leni wondered what the catch was. There had to be one, surely. Why *did* Giavanna want the dodo? Shoober looked confused too, as did Marion, Mimi and both professors.

"I've tried every anti-ageing treatment going," Giavanna said. "From rubbing coyote urine into my neck to bathing in hippo's milk. But nothing has worked..."

"Oh, I wouldn't say that," began Shoober weakly.

"Shuddup, you!" Giavanna snapped at her husband.

"By the way, you can do what you like with him," Giavanna told the cleaners. "I don't care. In fact, you'd be doing me a favour if you polished him off."

At this, Benny began to collapse, like a bouncy castle at the end of a party.

Leni couldn't believe it — Giavanna was even more vile than her husband, if that was actually possible.

"I never thought I'd see this day. But here it is. The

secret to looking young for ever is finally here. And it is mine! All mine."

"What are you talking about?" asked Leni. "What secret?"

"You're so young, my dear, such things don't matter to you. Let me fill you in," explained Giavanna. "When dodos were first discovered on Mauritius, centuries ago, we know that the European explorers sometimes ate them. But they also discovered that for those poor sailors suffering from scurvy, eating dodo eggs led to a miraculous recovery."

Professor Flowers looked dismayed. Professor Scissorson looked disgusted. And Leni looked at Giavanna in utter disbelief.

"Really?" she asked.

"Yes," said Giavanna. "It happened almost overnight. There was something in the eggs that turned scurvy-sufferers' skin from spotty and purply to glowing again, and their swollen and bleeding gums back to radiant smiles.

"And it gets even better," she went on. "Not only did

they cure their scurvy, but the explorers soon found that eating dodo eggs also had rejuvenating qualities — made them all look ten years younger! As you can imagine, the eggs became the most in-demand luxury food of the seventeenth century. But when dodos died out, so did the key to looking young for ever."

Professor Scissorson was shaking her head.

"As long as I can remember I've dreamed of trying a dodo egg," Giavanna declared. "But I never thought it would be possible... Until now."

Muppa had never mentioned anything about dodo eggs having anti-ageing effects and it sounded like a very tall story. Leni wondered where Giavanna had heard such nonsense.

"Now I will have an endless supply of eggs! I'll get a special hutch made, keep the dodo in my garden and eat her eggs whenever she lays them!" Giavanna gazed at the defenceless little bird. "And I will look young for ever!" She dangled Popcorn's cage and swung it from left to right, making him giddy on his perch.

"It's all rubbish," said Leni. "You've been told

a giant fib, Mrs Shoober." She felt sorry for this desperate woman.

"Hmph, well, you would say that, wouldn't you?" said Giavanna.

But Professor Flowers backed Leni up. "Leni's right, there's no truth in your story," he said. "You've been tricked, I'm sorry to say. Now if you'd just hand over the parakeet, we'll forget all about it — and you won't be left with egg on your face."

"Pah!" spat Giavanna. Then her face brightened again. "I'll have boiled dodo eggs with toasted soldiers, dodo egg and cress sandwiches and dodo egg omelette! Ha ha ha!" Her laugh could have grated cheese.

"Oh no you won't," cut in Professor Scissorson. "My dodo is a no-go."

"Oh really? And I suppose you don't want your friend the parakeet back?" threatened Giavanna. And with that she opened the cage door and took Popcorn out by the throat.

"If you don't give me the dodo, the parakeet gets it," she stated bluntly.

Giavanna tightened her grasp on Popcorn, making his eyes bulge and her knuckles whiten.

"Hand over the dodo, or I'll extinctify your little green friend," she hissed. "And I don't even care if it ruins my nails."

CHAPTER TWENTY-SIX

Dodo-a-go-go

Leni was torn. It would break her heart to lose the newly hatched dodo to this woman who'd stop at nothing to get what she wanted. But she couldn't stand by while Giavanna crushed Popcorn either.

Nearby, the molasses tank was bubbling away and the amber light was still flashing. Leni looked over to Shoober. The cleaners still had him firmly in their grasp. He was flinching, but running out of fight, like a fish out of water.

Professor Scissorson cupped the dodo in both hands, Professor Flowers bit his bottom lip and as for Popcorn, well, he looked as sick as a parrot.

"So?" said Giavanna, raising an overplucked eyebrow. "Which is it to be?"

Her perfume was so heavy and sweet, Leni could almost taste it.

"You do understand what I'm saying, little girl? If you don't give me the dodo I'll make your green friend go extinct," said Giavanna.

Leni looked at the defenceless dodo, then at poor Popcorn, and thought to herself, *What would Muppa do?*

But before she could come up with an answer to her own question, an ear-splitting siren rang out. It made Leni jump. It made them all jump. And in that critical moment, half a heartbeat at most, Giavanna let go of Popcorn.

"Argh!" she screamed, as the parakeet flapped his wings and tried to escape. "Who set off that wretched alarm?"

Popcorn's claws got caught in Giavanna's big hairdo and he desperately tried to break free while she desperately tried to recapture him. Finally, he disentangled himself and wasted no time flying over to Leni's shoulder.

His eyes returned from bulging to beady again — and Giavanna was left with hair like a bird's nest.

"The alarm went off automatically," said Professor Flowers, checking the gauge on the side of the molasses tank. The amber light had now started to flash red. "There's a malfunction — most likely triggered by the mops jamming up inside the centrifuge, causing fermentation and a build-up of pressure inside the tank," he continued. Then, turning to Leni, he announced, "We've got to get out of here." His voice sounded calm but his eyes told a different story. "Now."

Giavanna brushed the hair from her eyes and made a last-ditch lunge at the dodo chick, but Leni was too quick for her. She stuck out her foot and tripped up the wicked woman by her leopard-print boots so she stumbled and fell, and in a flurry of tangled hair and pink Lycra, she landed on top of Pawpaw and Beanbag.

"I don't want to alarm you, but the tank's about to explode," Professor Flowers called out in a shaky voice.

But there was one more thing Marion wanted to do before they made a run for it. "So, Mr

Shoober, your wife is fed up of you, is she? Well we're happy to do the dirty work for her."

Marion grabbed a plunger from inside the giant sugar bag and squelched it straight onto Shoober's bald head. She tightened her grip on the handle and spun him round again and again.

"Stop! Stop! Owwww!" howled the tycoon.

But Marion was having too much fun. "I've always wanted to take the plunge, and now I am!" she exclaimed.

Quickly, Leni wrapped the precious dodo chick in Professor Flowers's owl hanky and passed her to Professor Scissorson, who placed her gently into her shirt pocket. Then Leni, the professors and the cleaners made a dash for the door. In the heart of the factory, the molasses tank was starting to tremble and a dull rumble was getting louder, drowned out only by the sound of the siren.

Professor Flowers tried the door but it was jammed. "We're locked in," he gulped, pushing harder and harder at the door handle.

Could it be all over — just when they'd almost made it?

Leni stepped forward and pulled the handle.

"Oh," said Professor Flowers sheepishly as the door opened.

"You silly goose!" laughed Professor Scissorson when they burst into the outside world again.

"What can I say? Once a bird brain, always a bird brain," shrugged Professor Flowers.

"Come on, to the jeep!" shouted Professor Scissorson. "Follow me!"

CHAPTER TWENTY-SEVEN

Masses of Molasses

Leni, the professors and the cleaners tore along the gravel drive of Shoober's mansion, and down towards the iron gates as fast as their legs would carry them.

Leni led the way to the hidden jeep and jumped into the back, while Marion and Mimi sat either side of her and Popcorn perched on the frame.

Professor Scissorson clambered into the driver's seat and started the ignition.

"Wait for me!" panted Professsor Flowers. As he scrambled into the passenger side, the rumbling inside the factory started to get even louder. Then suddenly, a *pop! pop! pop!* sound peppered the air, like a giant popcorn machine turned up to maximum poppage power.

Professor Scissorson plunged the jeep into gear. The vehicle roared to life, just as an almighty explosion met their ears. It made the ground shake under their wheels.

Leni turned round to see what was going on behind them. And it was not a pretty sight.

The wild-haired Giavanna was running down the driveway, followed by the plunger-headed Shoober. They were both screaming in terror — probably because they were being chased by a fast-flowing river of molasses. It was slicking down the driveway at an alarming speed and already had the mansion in its gloopy grip.

Leni yelled back to their getaway driver. "As fast as you can, Professor Scissorson!" she called. "It's coming this way!"

Professor Scissorson floored the accelerator on the jeep and they sped off. Professor Flowers clutched the inside door handle and soon they left the treacly torrent far behind them.

"Eat our dust!" cried the cleaners in triumph.

"We got out of there just in time," said a relieved Professor Flowers.

"Those rotters got what they deserved," laughed Marion.

"They were as bad as each other," added Mimi.

"How could they even think about taking my precious dodo?" said Professor Scissorson.

"How is she, by the way?" asked Leni.

The professor checked her shirt pocket. "Good," she replied.

"Good!" squawked Popcorn. He looked happy to feel the wind in his feathers once again.

Professor Scissorson had to swerve to avoid a giant tortoise crossing the road. And then Professor Flowers began explaining the finer details of the chemical reactions that had caused the explosion in the molasses tank.

But Leni was in another world. Professor Flowers's words washed over her and she barely noticed the bumpy ride back. She was just relieved they'd escaped with both the dodo and Popcorn intact.

Not long afterwards they came to a halt. "Oh we're back are we? Well thank you, Professor Scissorson." The English man smiled at her.

"You're welcome," she replied. "And by the way, you can call me Celia."

CHAPTER TWENTY-EIGHT

First Name Terms

Leni had never been so glad to be back at Baie de la Vie, and she bounded up to hut 603. As soon as Professor Scissorson unlocked the door, she burst in.

"Loretta and Lionel, we have someone for you to meet!" called Leni.

They all trooped into the indoor aviary and gathered in the pigeon-playground in front of the birds' cubbyholes. The professor removed the little dodo hatchling from her pocket, still wrapped in Professor Flowers's hanky, and passed her to Leni. Then she took Loretta and Lionel from their pigeonholes and brought them out to meet their new daughter.

Leni carefully introduced the squab to her new mum and dad. Going beak-to-beak, the pink pigeons cooed over the baby dodo.

"Look, they're bonding," said Leni.

"Sweet," said Professor Scissorson.

Then the other pink pigeons started cooing too, like a gaggle of adoring aunties and uncles.

The cleaners broke into applause and Marion had to pass Mimi a tissue as she was getting teary. "She's gorgeous," said Marion. "You must be so proud."

"I couldn't have done it without your help, ladies.

In fact, without all your help," replied the professor.

Later, Professor Scissorson held a celebration party by making a small campfire on the beach and inviting them all to enjoy a mug of tea brewed in a billycan on the fire.

Professor Flowers took a sip. "It's delicious, Celia," he remarked. His glasses started to steam up, so he took them off and put them in his top pocket.

"It's how I brew it back home," replied Professor Scissorson. She opened a can of biscuits and offered him one. Then, looking like she wanted to say something important, she took a deep breath.

"I want to thank you, Professor Flowers, for all…"

"Please, Celia," interrupted Professor Flowers. "Call me Jethro."

"Jethro!" chirped Popcorn. The old man looked at the bird. "You stay out of it," he teased.

"Right-o," smiled Professor Scissorson nervously. "Well, Jethro, I just want to say that I am sorry I doubted you. I never in a million years thought you would help me and then when you showed up at the factory, I...I...well I just didn't think you had it in you."

"You underestimated me, didn't you?" said Professor Flowers, chuckling. He dunked his biscuit into his tea.

"I did," she admitted. "Actually I'm ashamed to say it now, but at one stage I thought it was you who had stolen the egg."

Leni wondered how Professor Flowers would take this, and not surprisingly, he looked hurt. "Listen, Celia," he replied. "We may have had our differences over the years but there's no way I would steal..."

"I know that now, of course and I am sorry," she said.

"It's okay," said Professor Flowesrs quietly. "I realize we haven't always seen eye to eye." He slurped his tea.

"Eye to eye!" squawked Popcorn loudly. He was sitting on Leni's shoulder, and enjoying all this.

"I know, Jethro. I was feeling sorry for myself. I was jealous."

"Well, that's very big of you, Celia. Thank you," said Professor Flowers.

"But," she added, "I have been wondering — how did you all work out that Leni and I were at Shoober's mansion?"

Professor Flowers wiped away some biscuit crumbs from his moustache. "I injected an egg with some dodo DNA — though I can't remember exactly which one. I had six, you see.

"Anyway, I put them all in cubbyholes, hoping that the pigeons might still sit on them. And, I was delighted to find that they all did. Each of the eggs was adopted by a pigeon who duly sat on it.

"Now I just had to watch and wait. This morning, I spotted the cleaners' buggy outside your hut, Celia, so I decided to clear off so I wouldn't be in their way when they came to my place. I thought a quick outing to stretch my legs and do a spot of birdwatching would be just the ticket."

The professor cleared his throat. "As I was walking down the road," he continued, "I heard a strange sound. A sort of muffled shriek, coming from somewhere within the woods. At first I thought it might be a Mauritius bulbul. But then I wandered into the woods and who should I find but Marion and Mimi? Well, I couldn't believe it."

"Believe me, we were very grateful to see you," said Mimi.

"We were tied up under a tree — those horrible men had bound and gagged us," said Marion. "They stole your egg, Professor Scissorson, and then they returned to swap back the golf buggy for their faster getaway car."

"They weren't very smart though," continued Mimi. "They couldn't resist bragging about stealing the egg and blurted out who their boss was. And everyone knows where the Sugar King lives."

"As soon as I realized those ghastly goons had your egg, Celia, I didn't think twice," said Professor Flowers. "It didn't matter any more who was going to de-extinct the dodo first. I just knew we had to try and get it back."

"The three of us jumped into the buggy and hit the road," said Mimi. "To be honest we'd have been there sooner, but it was an uphill ride."

"In a golf buggy," Marion reminded them.

"We thought we'd never get there," Mimi went on. "At one point we were overtaken by a wasp."

"But you made it," said Leni. "Just in time, too."

"And it's thanks to you all," said Professor Scissorson, "that the dodo is here with us now."

Suddenly they were interrupted by a hullabaloo coming from Flowers's hut. It sounded like the pigeons were causing pandemonium inside.

"What's all that cooing about?" wondered Leni.

Professor Flowers set down his mug of tea in the sand and stood up. "I don't know, but I'm going to find out," he said.

CHAPTER TWENTY-NINE
Squabbling

Professor Flowers left the campfire gathering and went to see what all the fuss was about inside hut 187.

A few moments later, they heard him call out, "Come here, all of you! You're not going to believe this!"

They all raced across the sand to his hut. Inside, the professor's books, papers and lab equipment were scattered around in total chaos.

"Oh my word!" said Professor Scissorson, clasping her hand to her collarbone.

"I know!" cried Professor Flowers. He reached down and picked up a green book from the floor. "My logbook! I've found it!"

"I meant the mess," said Professor Scissorson. "How can you work like this?"

Then Leni caught sight of something else. Something that explained what all the cooing was really about.

"Professor Flowers!" she whispered. "All of you, *look*!"

She pointed a quivering finger towards one of the pigeonholes on the top row of his loft. Everybody let out a gasp except Professor Flowers.

"What is it?" he asked, confused.

Leni had to remove his glasses from his top pocket and hand them to him.

Now he could see, along with the others, that sitting in the little cubbyhole, as bold as brass, was another little dodo squab.

"Two dodos in one day! Can it be possible?" cried Leni.

Professor Flowers peered through his specs at the miraculous bird, who was being tended to by its pigeon mum. When he realized what it was, he started crying with joy.

Like Professor
Scissorson's dodo,
this chick's eyes
were closed.
The mother
pigeon was fussing
over it and all the other
pigeons were cooing in delight.

"Look, it's getting milk from its mum," sniffed the
overjoyed professor.

"Milk?" said Mimi. "I didn't know pigeons could even
make milk."

"Well it's not milk exactly," explained Leni. "Pigeons
are one of the few bird species that produce a curd-like
substance in part of their digestive tract, a bit like milk.
Both parents produce it and they use it to feed their
babies."

"Well what do you know?" said an amazed Mimi.

The baby seemed to be thriving. So now there were
two dodos. Two! The news was still sinking in when
Leni felt a familiar tension in the air again. She noticed

Professor Flowers cast a glance over at Professor Scissorson while wiping away his tears of happiness. But also that Professor Scissorson was struggling not to burst into tears of despair.

They were both thinking the same thing, Leni realized. Whose dodo was first?

"Honestly, Celia, I am not trying to steal your thunder…" began Professor Flowers.

Profesor Scissorson composed herself. "You haven't stolen my thunder, Jethro," she replied curtly. "Obviously my dodo was first. Yours has only just this moment hatched."

"Well, we don't know exactly *when* it hatched, do we?" said Professor Flowers quickly. "After all, we've been chasing around after your dodo, saving her from a wretched calamity and…"

"Professors, stop! Both of you!" interrupted Leni. "It doesn't matter whose dodo hatched first," she said. "What matters is that there are two healthy dodos."

Just then the squab started fluffing out its downy grey feathers and flexing its legs, as if trying to strut. It was gaining confidence. "Well look at that," remarked Professor Flowers. "He's already ruling the roost."

"Do you think it's a male?" asked Leni.

"I'd say so," replied Professor Flowers.

"So if one's a boy and one's a girl, well…" Leni let her thought hang in the air.

The professors both looked awkward for a moment, and then Professor Flowers acknowledged it. "You're right, Leni. In evolutionary terms, a solo dodo is a no-go," he said.

He switched his attention to Professor Scissorson now. "In order for the species to continue, maybe, you know, Celia…we could…let them meet? See if they get on?" he suggested. "But only if you say so."

Leni knew that this plan would mean Professor Scissorson cooperating with Professor Flowers, but would she go for it?

"Come on, Celia, what do you say?" encouraged Professor Flowers. "Who knows, maybe there might even be more little dodos in the future."

"Oh, all right," said Professor Scissorson, extending

her hand. "Congratulations on your dodo, Jethro."

"Thank you, Celia, you won't regret it," said Professor Flowers, shaking on it.

"And, erm, keep up the good work. All right mate?"

"Indeed. Keep up the good work, old chum," Professor Flowers smiled.

"Well, you know the old saying," cheered a croaky voice behind them. "Birds of a feather, flock together."

They all turned around to see the silhouette of a small figure standing in the doorway, framed by the Mauritian sunlight.

"MUPPA!" yelled Leni. "You're back!" She raced over to her grandmother and gave her a huge hug.

"When I got your last letter I just knew I had to come home," said the old lady with a wide smile. "I didn't want to miss this moment for the world."

CHAPTER THIRTY

Freedom

The dodos grew bigger every day, and after a while the professors said that Leni could care for them. So she set up a special dodo suite in her tree house and with Muppa's help, she looked after the two thriving chicks.

The professors could have packed up their field labs and gone their separate ways, but they hung around, saying they wanted to stay on the island to do more important research.

"Do you think they'll ever leave?" said Leni to Popcorn and the dodos one morning. From the tree house they saw Professor Scissorson's leather hat lying on the chair outside hut 187.

Suddenly, the door to the hut opened and out came Professor Scissorson herself, carrying one end of her large wicker basket. She looked more relaxed than Leni had ever seen her before.

Leni climbed down from her tree and the moment Professor Scissorson spotted her, she shouted out, "Morning, early bird!"

Professor Flowers emerged from his hut holding the other end of the wicker basket. He was wearing a crisp white shirt and a Panama hat. "Ah my fledgling! How are you this bright day?" he called out.

"Hello, Professors. What are you doing?" Leni asked.

"We took the pink pigeons back to the sanctuary yesterday and now we're about to release Jethro's pigeons back into the wild," Professor Scissorson explained. "I'm giving him a hand."

Like a magician about to perform a dazzling trick, Professor Flowers said, "Celia, the hatch, please?"

Professor Scissorson released the little door on the top of the wicker basket and a flurry of flapping signalled the pigeons' freedom.

They darted about for a while, getting their bearings, rose and fell and finally whirled together in a big flock. They looked like doves, thought Leni. It was a moment of peace.

The birds soared through the warm currents of air, making their way inland until they got a bird's-eye view of the Shoober estate, sprawling out beneath them.

The smell of molasses hung heavy in the air. It had ruined everything and was still clinging to the windows, the roof, all down the front steps and most of the gardens.

On the ground, Pawpaw and Beanbag were clearing up the sticky mess. Right now, they were scraping molasses off the statue of Shoober with trowels.

"Nearly there," grimaced Beanbag.

"Done it!" declared Pawpaw with a grunt. He'd managed to scrape off the last of the gunk and stood there beaming.

"Good as new," sighed Beanbag, and the pair of them high-fived each other with their trowels.

Above them, the birds flocked together and did a couple of laps around the mansion. Then in perfect formation, they soared over the statue of Shoober and released a shower of pigeon poop right on his stony head.

CHAPTER THIRTY-ONE

Birds of a Feather

Professors Flowers and Scissorson shared their news in *The Quill*, the specialist magazine for bird scientists. In their article, they thanked Leni for all her help. Not only that, the Mauritian president awarded her a special "Bird Brain of Mauritius" medal. Her mum and dad were as proud as peacocks.

A few days later, the professors went to see Leni's family.

"We've really enjoyed our stay..." began Professor Flowers.

Leni's heart sank a little. Were they about to check out?

"So much so, that we'd like to stay even longer," cut in Professor Scissorson.

"That's lovely," said Leni's mum. "How long for?"

"Three months…" said Professor Flowers.

"…to start with," added Professor Scissorson.

"Wonderful! May I ask why?" queried Muppa.

"We've both been given the green light to go ahead and start trialling our de-extinction techniques on endangered birds here in Mauritius," said Professor Flowers. "And this time we're going to work together."

"Yes — we're starting with the Mauritius fody," announced Professor Scissorson, laying her hat on the kitchen table.

"Then we might get to work on the olive white-eye," added Professor Flowers. "A most interesting bird."

"Using the science we used to de-extinct the dodo — DNA capture and genome reconstruction and so on — we may be able to help to save these species before they go extinct," explained Professor Scissorson.

The dodos were growing fast and loved gambolling in the sand, strutting, waddling and generally doing what dodos used to do, all over again. During school hours, Muppa would dodo-sit, and then Leni would race home from her lessons to hang out on the beach with her two new friends.

"They're just like I imagined them," she said to Popcorn. "So adorable."

"Adorable!" he squawked. Was it just her or did he sound a bit jealous?

She stroked his green plumage. "Don't worry, Popcorn," she said. "You're still my favourite parakeet."

"It's easy to carry them up and down from the tree house at the moment," said Muppa. "But they're getting bigger. Soon it'll be trickier."

"It's just as well their proper home will be ready in a few weeks," replied Leni.

The dodos had had a special territory set aside for them, in the lagoon just off the coast of the main island of Mauritius. It was a small, wild island, uninhabited by humans and fringed with mangroves. It was perfect dodo terrain. Soon they'd be ready to roam, free of predators, and free from Benny and Giavanna Shoober's sticky hands.

Leni was busy learning all she could about the de-extincted birds and kept practising and improving her dodo-care skills.

"Go on, ask me anything," she said to Muppa one afternoon.

"Okay," Muppa replied. "A dodo chick with its beak in a net?"

"Settle it down and take to the vet."

"Fungal infection in the back of the throat?"

"Meds in their food is the antidote."

"A dodo with feathers that sometimes fall out?"

"That's moulting and nothing to worry about."

"Well I must say, these dodos are in good hands," laughed Muppa. She was in the middle of cleaning up some dodo poop from the floor of the tree house. The bottle's label read *The Splatomizer! Cleans up bird splodges, stains and smudges.*

"Marion and Mimi's spray is amazing," she said.

"Amazing!" repeated Popcorn.

Leni smiled. The cleaners had branded their formula into a special trigger-pump bottle, with a top shaped like a pigeon's head. The formula was still a closely-guarded secret, of course, but people loved how the fruity-fragranced spray came out of the pigeon's beak when they squeezed the trigger. Bottles and bottles rolled off the production line and supply could barely keep up with demand. Marion and Mimi were making a small fortune from *The Splatomizer!* — people were using it on everything from windscreens to wedding dresses.

The two dodos pecked at some Economy Pigeon Seed from Leni's hand. "You know, Leni, I've been thinking," Muppa went on. "I have a bit of money put aside. Just a little nest egg, you know. It's for you to have one day. It's not a fortune, but it'll be enough for you to build your own bird hospital."

"Wow, really?"

Muppa pulled a few stray leaves out of Leni's raven-black hair. "I'm so proud of you, Leni," she said. "I know you'll study hard, and once you've earned your wings and qualified as a vet, the money's all yours."

"Thank you, Muppa! One day I'm going to build a massive tree-house hospital. And I'm going to care for all the birds in it. Just wait and see!"

"Wait and see! Wait and see!" echoed Popcorn.

Birds

a poem by Leni

They chirp, they sing, they call, they gobble,

they squawk, they screech, they soar, they squabble.

From martins to mynas, fowl to flamingos,

I spot them out of my tree house window.

A company of birds, the early dawn chorus,

their eggs all oval and totally flawless.

They flit, they flock, they coo, they warble,

they're fancy-free and so adorable.

They preen, they peck, they pull and they push,
one in the hand is worth two in the bush.
They like eating insects or flowers or fruit,
birds live by their wits and they don't give a hoot.

They can migrate for miles, birds on the wing,
doing their own sweet birdy-like thing.
Those dino descendants are birds of a feather,
they light up my world and I love them for ever.

THE DODO LOWDOWN

Some fascinating facts about our feathered friends...

BOGGY BONES

In 1865, workers who were constructing a railway line in a marshy area of Mauritius called Mare aux Songes, unearthed dozens of dodo bones. These bones were sent to museums all over the world and helped experts to reconstruct skeletons of the extinct bird.

BIRDTIME STORY

In the same year, 1865, Lewis Carroll's classic story *Alice's Adventures in Wonderland* was published. It featured a fictional dodo and, as the book became popular, the extinct bird's fame increased.

DOUGH DOUGH

Some of Mauritius's bank notes feature
an image of the dodo.

TAKE A STAND

Dodos stood at a height of about one metre.

NOSING AROUND

In 2016, scientists scanned a dodo's skull and used it to
check out how its brain would have looked. From what
they saw, they figured that the bird would probably
have had a rather good sense of smell.

HOW'S YOUR DODO KNOW-HOW?

TAKE THE QUIZ TO DISCOVER HOW DODO-SAVVY YOU ARE

1: On which island did dodos live?

A) Majorca

B) Mauritius

C) Maui

2: To which type of bird are dodos most closely related?

A) Emus

B) Turkeys

C) Pigeons

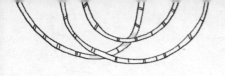

3: True or false? "The Dodo" was a bottom-wiggling dance craze which swept across Britain in the 1870s.

4: What's the scientific name for the dodo?
A) *Raphus cucullatus*
B) *Columba de Terra*
C) *Biggus Pigeonus*

5: True or false? Pigeon parents both produce a special type of "pigeon milk" to feed their chicks.

DODO JOKES TO CRACK YOU UP

How did the dodo pass her maths test?

She winged it.

Why did the chicken cross the road?

To get to the other side.

Why did the dodo cross the road?

To prove he was no chicken.

What did the dodo say to her misbehaving chick?

"You're grounded."

How did the dodo know he was about to moult?

He checked the feather forecast.

How do dodos send birthday cards?

By pigeon post.

What do you call two dodos living alongside
each other?

Nest-door neighbours.

What did the daddy dodo say to his son who was
sprucing up his feathers?

"I think that's enough preen time for today."

What do dodos spray under their wings to smell fresh?

Dododorant.

About the author

Fiona Sandiford has written for newspapers and
magazines in both the UK and Australia. She now lives
in Sussex with her family. She enjoys drinking strong
tea, listening to soul and disco music and stroking her
dog's ears. But perhaps her greatest love is making
mischief with words. *The Great Dodo Comeback*
is her first story for children.

About the illustrator

Clare Elsom is an illustrator of lots of popular children's books. She lives in Devon where she can be found drawing dodos, paddle boarding and having adventures with her young son.

FOR MORE CRACKING ADVENTURE STORIES
PLEASE VISIT USBORNE.COM/FICTION

USBORNE QUICKLINKS

The dodo is a famous example of an extinct animal. Although no extinct dodo has ever been brought back to life, scientists interested in de-extinction are working on ways to bring back lost species using preserved DNA.

For links to websites where you can find out more about the dodo, de-extinction and DNA, go to usborne.com/Quicklinks and type in the title of this book. Please follow the internet safety guidelines at Usborne Quicklinks. Children should be supervised online.